ghostgirl
Lovesick
by Tonya Hurley

Little, Brown and Company

New York Boston

Lyrics from "I Will Follow You into the Dark" (written and performed by Ben Gibbard, recorded by Death Cab for Cutie) © 2005 Atlantic Recording Corporation for the United States and WEA International Inc. for the world outside of the United States. Used By Permission. All Rights Reserved.

Lyrics from "Amerpsand" (written and performed by Amanda Palmer) © 2008 Eight Foot Music (ASCAP). All rights administered by Kobalt Music Publishing America, Inc. Used By Permission. All Rights Reserved.

Lyrics from "Kissing the Lipless" (written by James Russell Mercer and performed by The Shins) © 2003 Lettuce Flavored Music. Used By Permission. All Rights Reserved.

Lyrics from "Do You Love Me" (written by Nick Cave and performed by Nick Cave and the Bad Seeds) © 1994 Mute Song, Ltd. Used By Permission. All Rights Reserved.

☙☙

Little, Brown and Company

Hachette Book Group
237 Park Avenue, New York, NY 10017
Visit our website at www.lb-teens.com

First Edition: July 2010

Little, Brown and Company is a division of Hachette Book Group, Inc.
The Little, Brown name and logo are trademarks of Hachette Book Group, Inc.

Library of Congress Cataloging-in-Publication Data
Hurley, Tonya.
  Ghostgirl : lovesick / by Tonya Hurley.—1st ed.
    p. cm.
  Summary: Charlotte has been given her first assignment after graduating from Dead Ed—the alternative high school for dead teens—she is to go back and help out a student from her previous life and her first love, Damen.
  ISBN 978-0-316-07026-3
  [1. Future life—Fiction. 2. Friendship—Fiction. 3. Death—Fiction. 4. Ghosts—Fiction. 5. High schools—Fiction. 6. Schools—Fiction.] I. Title. II. Title: Lovesick.
  PZ7.H95667Ghu 2010
  [Fic] —dc22   2009029282

10 9 8 7 6 5 4 3 2 1

TTP

Book design by Alison Impey

Printed in China

For Michael

Chapter 1

I Touch Roses

And I kissed away a thousand tears
My lady of the Various Sorrows
Some begged, some borrowed, some stolen
Some kept safe for tomorrow
—Nick Cave

Memento mori.

Some people live their lives as if each day will be their last. Some approach love the same way, in a desperate attempt to outrun the tiny changes or huge ones that are always looming on each of our horizons. But the sense of urgency that comes from wanting to experience life and love to the fullest can force decisions that are not always in your best interests or anyone else's, for that matter. In fact, sometimes facing the consequences of your choices can be even worse than death. You may live only once, but you don't necessarily want it to feel like forever.

**carlet Kensington knew what she** was in for when she walked through the doors of Hawthorne High and was quickly overpowered by a sickly sweet floral aroma—the kind you smell only in a hospital room or funeral home.

"Valentine's Day," she sighed, partly from relief, partly from dread.

As she made her way to her locker, she couldn't escape the eye-watering aroma wafting from the cafeteria-tables-turned-makeshift-flower-markets, stationed like military checkpoints in every single hallway, alcove, and orifice. Students were selling "love" by the bunch. The fact that the flower sale was a fund-raiser only barely made it okay.

The girls were lined up buying the white roses, to give to their friends, and the guys were buying up the pink, mostly

so they wouldn't convey too much to the recipients, or more importantly to their "bros." They were more or less decoy roses for their on-the-down-low red ones. That was, unless they were lifers like a bunch of the business-track kids were — red roses sort of went hand-in-hand with school rings and pre-engagement pendants.

Valentine's had become more a season than a day, it seemed. Like Christmas and Halloween, it started earlier and earlier every year. In the past, Scarlet preferred to downplay it, viewing it as another irritating and overblown marketing ploy. She and her boyfriend, Damen, didn't need a prescribed day to declare their affection and exchange cards or candy, she had always thought.

Still, her feelings about it had softened lately. Even the scent of cheap flowers was slightly less offensive to her this year. It was a sweet tradition, after all, and, begrudgingly, she'd come to see the value in it. She was even smarting, ever so slightly, from the fact that Damen wouldn't be coming home from college to be with her, but this year Scarlet had another reason to partake in the lovefest.

Still, after a long day of seeing girls either scream with delight, huddle with their friends in giggle fits, or cry in the bathroom, Scarlet was ready for last period. She dumped her things in her locker and grabbed her anatomy textbook just as the bell rang. She headed to class, and because everyone was in a frenzy to purchase roses, she was one of the first to arrive. In the lab room, the floral smell, now mixed with formaldehyde, was nothing short of nauseating.

Her teacher, Mrs. Blanch, was pulling wet, dead cats from plastic bags, hence the smell of Valentine's Day dissected. Mrs. Blanch looked like a cat herself, with her dark eyeliner, pulled face, and salt-and-pepper beehive hairstyle. It was sort of like the way some people look like their dogs, Scarlet guessed. Science teachers sometimes resembled their experiments.

As class began, and Scarlet stared at the preservative-slick coats and long, uncertain incisions on the felines, all she could think of was how dead the cats really were, and yet they were still there. Present. She didn't think that the dissection thing was gross or even creepy necessarily, but it did seem undignified, especially considering this crew of rocket surgeons preparing to dig in. Who could forget the time Freddy Kunkle was suspended for eating a dead kitty kidney on a dare? So much for higher learning. And dead cats.

The band horn section was outside practicing "Lose Yourself in Me," by My Bloody Valentine, and provided just enough distraction and inspiration for Scarlet as she tuned out the junior varsity veterinarians and sat by the window doodling song lyrics in her notebook. She pretended to analyze the cat innards, poking at them like brussels sprouts whenever Mrs. Blanch was looking, and then returned to her notebook to jot down not scientific observations, but verses. The bell rang and she was first out and first in line at the flower table just outside the classroom.

She stopped and spent a few moments looking over the amateurish bouquets and corsages, then noticed a gorgeous,

heart-shaped wreath of garnet roses hanging behind the salesgirls.

"Hey, Marianne," Scarlet said to the girl manning the table.

"Hi, Scarlet." Marianne smiled cheerily. "What can I get for you?"

Marianne Strickland was Hawthorne's leading band fund-raiser and an expert in chirpy, superficial sales-speak. In fact, she carried around candy cartons more often than her instrument. So it was no surprise to Scarlet she'd be drumming up flower sales to purchase much-needed spit valves for the brass section. She took her responsibilities very seriously, and Scarlet admired her dedication.

Before Scarlet could get another word out, Lisa McDaniel, who was voted funniest girl in the senior class, popped up from underneath the table. Lisa irked Scarlet because the girl was much more annoying than funny; she was *yearbook funny*, Scarlet liked to say. In other words, she met a very low threshold of funny.

"Take my plants…please," Lisa, in an outfit as dated and goofy as her material and breath smelling of egg salad, joked eagerly. Scarlet was tempted to hiss out a rim shot but resisted and just ignored her.

"I love this wreath," Scarlet said warily. "How much?"

They were Ingrid Bergman roses on the wreath, Scarlet's favorite. Dark red fragrant hybrids with a bud that was almost black. She loved the hint of purple they picked up as they aged, but more importantly, she loved that they tended to live

quite a long while after they'd been cut. They were as beautiful and timeless as their namesake. Scarlet felt like a museum curator coming across a priceless antique brooch at a local flea market. She was sure these flower girls had no idea how special their flowers were.

"We made up that wreath to promote the sale," Marianne shot back in a no-nonsense tone, the imminence of a transaction wiping out her cheer. "We made it big and elaborate, so it would cost a lot if we were to sell it."

"I've only got thirty dollars with me," Scarlet said.

"We were thinking more like forty," Marianne said, involving Lisa in the negotiations, even though Lisa clearly had no clue.

"Can I get the rest to you tomorrow?"

Despite the fact that Scarlet's popularity had unwittingly grown to unfathomable proportions and she was now off the scale when it came to cool, she knew already what Marianne's response would be.

"Scarlet, if I do it for you," Marianne explained judiciously, "I'd have to do it for everyone and I can't spend my days chasing down money."

"I got your back!" Lisa McDaniel exclaimed, laughing herself into a tizzy as she dropped ten dollars into the till.

"Thanks, Lisa," Scarlet said with genuine surprise.

Scarlet handed the rest to Marianne and tossed the wreath over her shoulder like a handbag. For a band-made arrangement, it was lovely. There must have been a hundred roses packed tightly together in an infinite, lush heart.

Anywhere else, one of these would go for seventy-five bucks, at least.

"For Damen?" Lisa asked sheepishly, hoping for a little gossip in exchange for her loan.

Scarlet looked at the girls, smiled knowingly, and walked toward her locker to grab some things and then leave. The flowers *were* for Valentine's Day, but they weren't for Damen.

⋙⋘

Winter had nearly run its course, but not completely. There were few telltale signs of changing seasons, at least none that were external or obvious—still no grass growing, trees greening, or flowers budding. The ground was still soft and sloppy from recent downpours, the air damp and cold, the mid-February sky cloudy and gray.

The breeze was cold against her skin, but luckily she was dressed for it. Scarlet, toting her floral wreath across town, was shawl-ready, wrapped from shoulder to knees in a black and violet plaid Scottish wool throw. It was a good thing too; the wind always picked up at the cemetery.

She approached the enormous, black wrought-iron gates at the end of town that sported the Greek letter alpha on one side and omega on the other. They were open just wide enough to let a person pass, and Scarlet walked through, her sharp black-clad silhouette seeming almost to become part of the ironwork. She continued up the dirt path, occasionally sloshing through small puddles left by the rain.

The first thing she noticed was that she was alone except for the groundskeeper, which affected her in a deeper way than

she would have expected. Given the weather, and the fact that visiting hours were nearly done for the day, it was not surprising, but the sudden sense of solitude was very noticeable.

There are two kinds of people, Scarlet immediately thought—those who visit graves the way she did and those who don't. She didn't think any less of those who don't. Usually they had very good reasons, most of them having to do with wanting to remember the person as he or she had lived. At least that's what they said, but more likely it was due to the inconvenience of the trip.

Scrapbook people, she considered them, who preferred to flip through photos of the deceased at home and reminisce rather than trek out to the boneyard. They were generally the same people who sent longwinded computer-printed notes on homemade stationery with their Christmas cards. People who appeared to be overly sentimental, but were just hypocrites, as far as Scarlet was concerned. They were only in it for the attention.

Of course there was always the most obvious and often unspoken reason: they were just afraid. Scared of the rows and rows of neatly organized corpses and the mounds of loose dirt that covered them. And, ultimately, frightened of the inevitable truth that the cemetery represented their own fragility and mortality. It was all about them in the end, she thought, not the poor soul who'd gone to rest. But then, what wasn't?

As she trod through the rows of marble, her feet sticking slightly in the mud, she could see, a short distance away at the very back of the cemetery, a clearing, or at least a much less

crowded patch of ground. Scarlet walked directly toward it, leaving the road and cutting across the graves, apologetically patting each headstone as she passed.

As her shadow, enlarged and elongated by the setting sun, crossed the graves, Scarlet saw the inky outline of her A-line skirt, and her cape blowing. Her hair had grown out from an asymmetrical razor-cut bob to a long, flowing Bettie Page. She appeared, to herself, so streamlined, so adult.

She was wearing her vintage Wellies with a gorgeous drab, smoky teal tulle dress from a local thrift store. Scarlet made it her own by cinching it together with a big thick men's leather belt. She was still a feminine hipster all the way, straight out of a magazine, the other kids would whisper; but she knew she was different now, inside and out. Gone were the strategically ripped leggings, ragged skirt, layered tees, bright red matte lipstick that once defined her style. They were all gone. Gone like her anger and cynicism. Gone like Charlotte.

It had happened slowly, imperceptibly, like the Freshman Fifteen. It was as if her closet was at war with itself, the older, edgy pieces losing ground to the tailored ones. A genuine style-off: The Karen O against the Jackie O. Scarlet hadn't taken sides in the wardrobe war, but Damen seemed to be Jackie O all the way. Though she hated to admit it, that kind of positive reinforcement and approval from him was atypically influential these days. Ever since her sister Petula's near-death experience from her pedicure-induced coma and Scarlet's own adventure on the Other Side, Scarlet had really come to value

the people around her. Even her big sister. And what they thought mattered to her.

Scarlet slowed as she approached the single white marble headstone just a few yards before her. Unlike the other headstones in the cemetery, this one hadn't tarnished yet. She was relieved to find it in such good condition because she hadn't seen it since before the holidays. The truth was, Scarlet was one of those nonvisitors until recently. Until she'd spent the entire fall raising money for this headstone for Charlotte.

It was even more beautiful than when she'd ordered it, she thought, bending slightly to run her hand across the engraving of Charlotte's name and legend. She stood upright again, eye-to-eye with the sculpted portrait she'd commissioned to sit atop the stone. It was an ethereal image of Charlotte that Scarlet had designed—eyes gazing thoughtfully, lips smiling slightly, long hair flowing.

It was only fitting, she thought, that Charlotte be memorialized in this way. Pictures in the school lobby and yearbook, classroom tributes by ghost-hunter-obsessed teachers were not permanent enough to commemorate Charlotte, Scarlet remembered thinking at the time. It was the least she could do, since Charlotte never really had a proper funeral, given her whole family—or lack thereof—situation.

Damen was so proud of Scarlet for doing it, and she even drummed up a lot of unexpected support from the student body, comprised mostly of students who wouldn't have known Charlotte if they'd tripped over her. Even Petula made a

small personal donation, which was very unlike her, but much appreciated, given her massive popularity. The Wendys, her sister's two-faced toadies, were the last to contribute, and they made a single donation in both their names, which was both obnoxious and fitting. Scarlet figured they were afraid of being haunted and ponied up as a sort of investment in their shared peace of mind.

Scarlet concentrated on the carving for a long while, trying to determine how much it actually resembled Charlotte. She ran her hand gently and deliberately along the chiseled curves of Charlotte's cheek, her brow, her nose, her lips—features she literally knew like the back of her own hand. She wondered what Charlotte would think of the tribute.

Charlotte's life really had been short, and she was going to miss all the changes that, for better or worse, are a part of growing up and growing old. It occurred to Scarlet for the first time since she'd visited Charlotte on the afterlife intern campus that this might be the only place she'd ever see Charlotte again.

It seemed as good a place as any to leave Charlotte, well, mail, Scarlet thought, pulling a damp, sealed white no. 10 envelope from her bag. A stamp seemed unnecessary. She was pretty sure that Charlotte was one place the post office wouldn't deliver. Instead, she put it in a plastic bag and tied the bag tightly to one of the thorny rose stems. Good enough.

She raised the heart-shaped arrangement, framing Charlotte lovingly in the center of it, gently draped the wreath

around her swanlike neck, and stepped back to admire the beauty of both. Scarlet bent down, as if to pray, but instead pressed her hand down, leaving her handprint in the moist soil.

"I hope you're okay," she whispered sincerely, then got up and plodded away.

Chapter 2

Kiss Them for Me

*Whisper you mean it, say you'll stay
Hold my heart till brighter days
— Bat for Lashes*

Sometimes you have to go it alone.

———◆◆◆———

No guts, no glory. Like a kamikaze, there are times when you may be required to leave the life you knew behind and give it over to a greater purpose. The costs can be high, to your heart, soul, and reputation. Whether or not what you gain will ultimately outweigh what you gave is impossible to know, and really irrelevant. Your comfort comes in the knowledge that some things are worth sacrificing for.

harlotte," a gentle voice called out, "It's time to wake up now."

"Wake up?" Charlotte thought, still groggy and submerged in sleep.

The voice was sweetly familiar, one that she had archived in her memory as well as her heart but that still could only barely penetrate the wall of sleep she'd built around herself. It seemed to come both from everywhere and no place in particular. Charlotte felt it more than she heard it, and she'd been "feeling" it much more often now that she was so prone to oversleeping.

"Come on," the voice pleaded a bit more urgently. "You're going to be late."

As Charlotte came to, she realized that she really hadn't been sleeping so much as resting. Not for the sake of her

body—that need had passed along with her life—but for her mind. She was happier than she'd ever been, but also nervous, jittery, and preoccupied, the way you feel whenever a major change approaches.

It was the kind of feeling of both relief and expectation she'd had at the end of every school year. No more pencils, no more books. No more teachers, classmates, hall monitors, lunchroom ladies, bus drivers, or dirty looks. Summer was coming, full of freedom and possibility. The only difference now was that summer could last forever. In fact, she was counting on it.

"Charlotte Usher! Get up this minute!"

Charlotte's eyes flung open as if a ripcord had pulled them. She looked around the room and let out a sigh of relief.

I'm still here, Charlotte thought. *It's all still here.*

It was the same thing every morning. She would hear the voice and then question if it was real or if everything was just some crazy dream. If she were still alive, she might have thought she was becoming demented, but the nice thing about being dead was that she didn't have to worry about losing it. So, scratch that.

Maybe, Charlotte thought, it was just that she'd been filled with longing, even pain, for so long that she wasn't used to being happy. Not that she was one hundred percent elated all the time, though. As wonderful as her reunion with her parents had been, it had come with certain disadvantages. She'd gotten used to being alone and had always prized her autonomy, which was more and more in dispute these days. She was increasingly accountable now, not only to her parents, but also

to her intern supervisor, Markov, and the hotline hysterics. It was a lot of change to process.

"Charlotte!" the voice rang out again, this time in a tone that was very, very real.

"I'm up!" she yelled, pulling the drapes back.

The only thing that made waking up easier these days was the knowledge that it would all be over soon—the early mornings, the depressing phone calls, and the responsibility. Today was the last day at the afterlife intern office.

"Charlotte, sweetheart," her mother spoke as she planted herself down on her bed, "Is everything, you know, okay?"

Her mother wanted so much to impart wisdom whenever she could, seeing as she'd missed out on a lifetime of it, but she'd learned not to press too hard. They hadn't had the day-to-day conflicts that plague many mother-daughter relationships, but that didn't change the fact that there was still a warehouse full of emotional baggage that Charlotte had yet to unpack. And more than a carry-on of it was family-related.

Charlotte turned slowly from the window and faced her. "Mom?" she asked, as if she wanted to hear herself say it but still wasn't used to it.

"Yes, monkey puff?" Eileen eagerly replied, with just a trace of worry in her voice. She tried to make up for a life-time of terms of endearment, which often resulted in mushy mash-ups.

Charlotte took a deep breath and her eyes widened.

"Never mind," she said, and hurriedly headed for the door. "Love you."

"Love you too," Eileen called after, the closing front door clipping her farewell and their conversation.

☙

On the way to the intern office, Charlotte picked up Pam and Prue, just as she did each morning. They were old friends by now, honest with each other to a fault. The no-holds-barred girl talk, which was as eye-opening as a cup of espresso, was always the best part of her day. As they walked, Charlotte filled them in on her morning.

"Don't you feel comfortable enough with her yet to open up about your boyfriend?" Pam asked.

Pam was hoping Charlotte's mom might drum some sense into her about Eric, the new boy she'd been "dating."

"Did she try to have 'the talk'?" Prue asked, bursting into laughter.

Charlotte felt bad about the fact that she had never gotten "the talk" or even had a reason for it until now.

"I just didn't feel like discussing my love life with my mother, that's all," Charlotte said as they made their way to the phone bank once more. "It's just weird."

"Is it because he's older?" Prue teased.

"He's not really older," Charlotte said. "We're almost the same age; he's just been dead longer."

"Oh, well, that explains it," Prue sneered sarcastically.

The fact that he'd been dead longer was actually a big part

of his appeal to Charlotte. She'd always thought of herself as an old soul, even when she was alive, and there was a realness about Eric that she found missing in most guys she'd known, Damen excluded, of course. Eric was a throwback to another time, not very long ago, in fact; and that, to her, was not a bad thing.

"Have you kissed him?" Pam asked, wanting to hear some juicy, revealing details.

"Don't encourage this, Pam," Prue jumped in. "You know she can't have a *real* kiss with him."

"Maybe not a *living* kiss," Charlotte replied defensively, "but we can still be close."

Yet another downside of being dead, Charlotte thought.

"Do you love him?" Pam asked, poking around to see how far gone Charlotte was.

"Yeah, I think I do," Charlotte admitted out loud for the first time.

"But Charlotte," Pam chided. "You barely know him."

What Pam actually meant to say, Charlotte thought, *was we barely know him*. She was just being protective, as a good friend should be. The fact that Eric had transferred in after they'd arrived, pretty much taking that sneaky saboteur Maddy's open seat, made the other interns a little suspicious, no matter how nice he seemed. That he had been a musician in life didn't exactly score him a lot of brownie points with Pam and Prue either.

"Never mind him," Prue said, skeptically. "What do you know about *love*?"

It was a fair question, but not one that Pam or Prue could answer either, and Charlotte knew it. Not that it stopped them from badgering her.

"I don't *know* anything about it," Charlotte shot back. "But I know what I *feel*."

"Well, *I* feel like we've been down this road before," Prue barked, her disapproval showing.

"What is that supposed to mean?" Charlotte quizzed indignantly.

"It means you're carrying on just like you did with Damen," Pam said. "You're obsessed. Again."

"Look where that got you," Prue reminded. "And this guy is no Damen."

Charlotte held her tongue and thought for a second about what the girls were trying to tell her. It was true; Eric was nothing like Damen on the outside. Actually, he was almost the exact opposite. The way he dressed, his lifestyle, his ambitions. Not the kind of guy Charlotte would ever have considered as a soul mate.

She'd gotten to know him though — the real him, she liked to say. And underneath the leather, chains, and spiky hairdo, Eric was sweet and kind. He was also monopolizing more and more of her free time, which is what Charlotte thought this whole chat was really about anyway.

"I think you're both jealous," Charlotte fired back. "That I finally found someone."

"Don't be so defensive," Pam said. "We're just looking out for you."

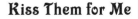
"I'm not being defensive," Charlotte complained. "But here I am telling you how happy I finally am and you're both lecturing me like I'm a child."

"Maybe that's because you still haven't learned your lesson," Pam chided.

"Which is?" Charlotte pressed.

"Love is for the living," Pam answered. "It's one of the first discussions we ever had, remember?"

"You said that's why they call it a love *life*," Charlotte recalled. "I remember."

"You've made so much progress," Pam said sweetly, "and now you're jeopardizing it for a guy you just met."

Everyone took a breath to reload. Pam and Prue knew Charlotte well enough to know that she was nowhere near ready to concede.

"I know he got electrocuted onstage by his own amp while he was playing his music in a storm," Charlotte dug in. "He definitely understands commitment."

"Maybe he should have understood a little more about meteorology," Prue cracked.

"That's mean," Charlotte said. "Why are you guys being so negative?"

"You have nothing in common with him," Prue went on. "He's a musician. A wanderer."

"Pam was a musician, too!" Charlotte retorted, realizing instantly it wasn't a very good comeback.

"Not like him," Pam joked, spreading her legs wide and turning a few air-guitar windmills to make her point.

"You make him sound so shady," Charlotte responded. "Like he has a girlfriend in every town or something."

"Maybe not, but I half expect to see groupie ghosts hanging all over him every time I look at him," Prue added for good measure.

Prue may have stepped over the line, but she was also persuasive. So far, Charlotte's relationship had been smooth sailing, but the girls were really raising some suspicions that she'd been harboring anyway. Eric did look like a guy with a reputation, but Charlotte couldn't decide whether that marked him as too easy or too hard to get.

"He just doesn't look like the type to settle down is all," Pam said, a little more sympathetically. "We don't want you to be disappointed or hurt."

"Guys are only as faithful as their options," Prue spouted. "Keep that in mind."

Since it was so new, Charlotte was still really sensitive about the relationship, and ordinarily she would have been angry and hurt at Prue's digs. But knowing Prue's history with guys, and how she died, Charlotte was willing to cut her some slack.

"I think that maybe this could be forever," Charlotte pondered hopefully. "You never know."

"Of course I do, Charlotte, and so do you," Pam said. "Everything has an expiration date."

"And everyone," Prue added. "We're proof of that."

"Everything," Charlotte admitted, "except love."

Pam and Prue just shook their heads in exasperation.

They clearly had not made a dent in Charlotte's stubborn romanticism.

The threesome arrived at the phone bank and were pleasantly surprised by how different everyone looked. Happy, rested, and at peace. Even CoCo had a relaxed air about her, and not from her flatiron either. After a few tears and hugs and kisses, Charlotte thought, they'd all be off for a hard-earned afterlife of leisure and an eternity with friends and family. They'd all remain close, of course, and if not, there would always be reunions, she was sure. That would be heaven.

The only downside for Charlotte was that she'd been getting to see Eric in the office every day. Now she'd have to be lucky enough to run into him around the compound or, just maybe, find another way to spend even more time with him. Charlotte scanned the room quickly—she didn't want to be obvious—and noticed his office was empty, along with Mike's and DJ's.

"Late again," Pam noted to Charlotte.

"Predictable to the end," Prue complained.

"Metal Mike and DJ are bad influences," Charlotte whispered, excusing Eric from blame. "Too many late-night jam sessions, that's all."

Markov cleared his throat, signaling for quiet. He was not the sentimental type, so no one expected a gooey farewell speech.

"I'm glad you are all here," Markov began. "Well, almost all of you."

As he was about to continue his remarks, the interns heard a familiar rumbling of footsteps that quickly grew into a stampede as what appeared to be a little tornado of souls burst in. They turned toward the door, overhung by the sign that read *Docendo discimus (We learn by teaching)*.

"Sorry, yo," DJ hollered.

"D.O.A.," said Mike.

"You're tardy," Markov admonished.

Just because it was their last day didn't mean he was going to give Eric, Mike, and DJ a pass. He considered tardiness not just disrespectful to him, but dangerous to all those callers who were counting on them for guidance.

"Oh," Eric said casually as he took his seat, in a tone that might have conveyed either arrogance or curiosity, depending on one's point of view. "Did we miss something important?"

Eric was rough around the edges, rocking a choppy punk haircut, Wayfarers, a black leather jacket, red high-tops, ripped skinny black jeans, and an attitude to match. He could be coarse but was always charming and hard to dislike. Even for Markov, who cracked a knowing smile.

"I'd like to think that everything I say is important," Markov replied sarcastically. "Otherwise I'd be wasting my breath."

"What breath," Eric joked, fist-bumping his cohorts.

"Now, may I proceed?" Markov asked sarcastically.

"Proceed," Eric proclaimed magnanimously.

Charlotte broke out into a wide grin at Eric's nerve. She could never be as willfully rebellious as he was, but she had

broken a few rules herself and could totally relate. Besides, she loved the way he slung his guitar over his shoulder and how his demo tape poked out of the top of his jacket pocket, ready to be handed over to someone who might give him his big break.

He still had dreams too, she thought. He glanced over at her and nodded a silent hello, locking eyes with her for just a second. To Charlotte, it felt like forever.

"Interns, your work here is done," Mr. Markov said, uttering the words they'd been longing to hear.

A collective sigh of relief escaped the interns' mouths.

"And just as we did upon your arrival here," Markov added, "we will celebrate with a surprise."

Markov gestured toward the doors and right on cue, they reopened, silently this time. Everyone was speechless, watching the new crop file through the doors.

"Your replacements," Markov declared.

They marched in one by one, all familiar faces. A new class of Dead Ed graduates ready to man the phones.

"Green Gary!" Pam yelled, waving him over.

"Holy shiitake," Gary called back.

Charlotte gave him a squeeze on his way over to Pam, and then noticed Paramour Polly, Lipo Lisa, Tanning Tilly, and the rest of them. She looked anxiously to see who would come in next. Her patience was rewarded.

The light that blazed through the doorway completely engulfed the last visitor, who stepped forward tentatively.

Charlotte watched as the light receded, little by little, exposing the petite, angelic figure passing through it.

"Virginia," Charlotte sighed as they both ran toward each other, smacking into a big bear hug.

Pam joined the hug. Prue tried to resist, but quickly gave in, grabbing hold of the others as they rotated around and around like a supernatural ceiling fan.

"How nice to see you all," Virginia greeted with total correctness, having internalized the formality that Petula had drilled into her during their short acquaintance.

She was quite the little lady now. Poised, polished, and pretty as ever. Maybe not older, but certainly wiser for her time with Petula and in Dead Ed. She was special.

"All right, people," Markov belted out to the interns, interrupting the festivities. "Gather your stuff."

"For?" Prue asked pointedly.

"A little trip," Markov answered vaguely.

A little trip sounds good, Charlotte thought, and judging from the smiles on everyone else's faces, they were thinking the same thing. CoCo began to plan her wardrobe immediately, and Call Me Kim, unable to restrain herself from spreading the good news, "dialed" her family.

"Vacation!" Pam yelled, hoping to kick things off spring break–style.

"Not exactly, Pam," Markov continued. "It's more like a business trip."

"We're going on the road," Eric exclaimed, with Mike and DJ high-fiving each other behind him like some wannabe roadies.

"But," Charlotte chimed in skeptically, "you said our work here was done?"

"That's right," Markov said, patronizing her just a little. "I said your work *here* was done."

"Then where?" Charlotte asked, not really wanting to hear the answer.

"Pack your mental baggage, people," Markov announced. "You're going back."

Chapter
3

Kill Your Darlings

Time is a dressmaker specializing in alterations.
–Faith Baldwin

Keep the change.

Holding on to someone you know you have to let go of is not just a way to delay the inevitable for them, but for yourself, as well. It protects you from having to make the transition you are about to impose until you are good and ready. Like canceling on an out-of-town guest you've been longing to see, but never quite had the time to plan for, it is the convenient, easy way out—for you.

on't you need a car seat for her?"
Wendy Anderson said, pointing to the
inconvenient bundle on Petula's lap.

"I don't like the way the shoulder straps crease her clothes,"
Petula replied, waiting until Wendy Anderson got situated in
the backseat before speeding off.

"Where's *your* kid?" Petula asked as if she were referring to
an unwanted appendage.

"Day care," Wendy Anderson snipped.

"Hey, put her socks on; they're falling off. She needs that
pop of pink or else her look won't work," Petula said to Wendy
Thomas in the front seat.

Wendy pulled the baby's socks up, but they weren't straight
or even an equal distance above each ankle.

"Do I have to do *everything* myself?" Petula asked in a huff
as she carefully fixed them just so.

This baby doll assignment had become quite popular at Hawthorne as a way of teaching responsibility and counteracting at least a little of the rampant selfishness among students. Considering the battered and stained condition that most of the dolls were returned in, the jury was still out on the experiment.

"Did you write down in the log what your parasite ate last night?" Wendy Thomas asked Petula.

"No, because she didn't eat. She barely fits into the clothes I just bought her, so she's detoxing," Petula said casually. "I won't have a baby with a baby bump."

The Wendys were surprised that Petula, in her own way, cared so much about her baby, at least about how she looked anyway. It opened the door to a discussion they'd been having.

"Funny you should mention the whole baby fat thing," Wendy Anderson added.

"We were thinking that the next big trend could be baby lipo," Wendy Thomas continued. "We could collect the lard and then use it as a renewable biofuel for cars and buses."

"It addresses both our foreign oil dependency and epidemic childhood obesity," Wendy Anderson added. "It's eco-friendly too."

Petula was unfazed by The Wendys' industriousness; in fact, she was barely even listening to them. She was too distracted by the sight of a homeless woman lingering over a Dumpster behind the organic supermarket. Rather than speed away, Petula slowed down and eyed the vagrant as an archer does a bull's-eye. The Wendys readied to ridicule. If Petula was going

to take the time to acknowledge her existence, both girls surmised, they'd better be prepared to mock.

"That's horrible," Petula said.

"It rots," Wendy Thomas said, using all of the protein-bar derived energy she could muster to stop her gagging reflex.

"At least she's trying to eat healthy," Wendy Anderson giggled cruelly.

"Shut it!" Petula commanded, pulling over even closer to the depressing scene. "You two couldn't walk an inch in her shoes."

"What shoes?" came the clueless query from Wendy Thomas, which was met by stony silence from Petula.

The Wendys locked eyes conspiratorially. The truth was, Petula had been acting very different since she "came back" from her near-death experience, and they were growing increasingly wary of her, even before this outburst. They expected *some* changes, but they were thinking more along the lines of a semi-dead accent or a more svelte figure thanks to the liquid-only IV diet that coma patients were lucky enough to require, not these wild mood swings, which weren't obvious to a layman, but to Petula-acolytes like them were huge.

Still, they mostly chalked it all up to something she picked up while she was away, odd conduct that was most likely a direct result of her pseudo-passing. Besides, Petula didn't talk about the whole experience much. They weren't sure if it was because she didn't remember anything or because it was part of a "what happens in the afterlife stays in the afterlife" pact.

Alternatively, it could just be P.P.D.—pre-prom delirium. The Wendys thought that was a more acceptable "diagnosis,"

and they were confident that the few weeks they spent in and out of the hospital when Petula was a patient medically qualified them to come to such a conclusion.

Petula stopped the car, spritzed some sugary body spray on the bottom of her shirt, and pulled it up over her glossed lips like a surgical mask to defend against the smell of urine. She got out and approached the woman. The Wendys were amazed. They'd kept the windows rolled up tightly to keep the heat in and the stench out, so the brief chat was impossible to overhear. But the fact that Petula was talking to this person at all was really the issue. Evidence was mounting. Her condition was worsening.

"What is she doing?" Wendy Thomas asked.

"You know, when they diagnosed my grandmother with Alzheimer's, all her other medical stuff disappeared. The doctor said that sometimes people forget they're sick and so things resolve," Wendy Anderson said.

"What are you talking about?" Wendy Thomas asked, quickly losing her patience. "What do you know about anything?"

"I know lots of things…like, there is a stunningly high suicide rate tied to reality TV show contestants, oh, and, you can wallpaper an entire room with the tissue of just one lung…," Wendy Anderson spouted off proudly. "And, I know that my grandmother had diabetes, got Alzheimer's, and then forgot she had diabetes and so did her body. It might be the same here. Petula's near-death might have, you know, given her popularity amnesia."

"That's genius!" Wendy Thomas said sincerely. "I don't

know why everyone is so shocked that you were accepted to online college for next year."

Petula got back in the car, fully aware of what The Wendys were thinking, and moved quickly to defuse the situation.

"What was that about?" Wendy Thomas asked accusingly.

"I asked her where she got that scarf she was wearing," Petula spouted, feigning indignance. "It looked just like one that might have fallen out of my car last week."

The Wendys accepted the explanation for the time being, but Petula was angry that she'd let herself get carried away like that. This kind of schizophrenic behavior was getting harder for her to keep under wraps. She could neither understand nor control it.

As soon as Petula pulled away from the curb, Wendy Anderson received a foreboding emergency text.

"Petula," she said, "you aren't going to like this."

"Out with it," Petula demanded.

"Someone spotted that transfer student, Darcy, wearing the same sweater that you have on now!" Wendy Anderson chirped, fishing for a reaction.

Petula made what she was wearing a status update on each of her social networking sites every day so that no one would wear the same thing that she had on. Everyone knew that, except, apparently, for the new girl. Or maybe, Petula was thinking, it was intentional.

"It's the same color too," Wendy Thomas added. "Reportedly."

Petula had nothing but hate for Darcy, even though she didn't really know her, and no one seemed to know much about the new girl, except that she'd recently come to Hawthorne

from Gorey High. That on its own was enough to put her right at the top of Petula's Out list, but she'd had a bad feeling about Darcy since she'd arrived at Hawthorne. It was a gut feeling, much like her instinctive aversion to buying jewelry from the home shopping channels. The Wendys, on the other hand, may not have liked Darcy either, but they secretly liked that Petula was threatened by her.

Petula pulled over, stopped the car again, got out, and opened the trunk, which was filled with plastic bags packed with clothes of all sorts. One more thing to alphabetize in the "crazy file," The Wendys thought. It was becoming pretty clear that Petula was two garments short of a runway show.

"Was the dry cleaner's closed?" Wendy Anderson called out the rear window.

"My closets are bursting and I think Harlot is stealing my clothes," Petula offered. "I don't want to leave anything lying around."

The Wendys nodded in unison and waited patiently in the car. This seemed plausible. Scarlet had been looking better lately, they grudgingly admitted to themselves.

Petula rifled through the bags until she found a suitably fashionable and competitive change of clothes, pulled off her crewneck sweater, and right there on the street replaced it with a plum-colored cashmere cardigan. She was never worried about making a public display of her assets because Petula believed wholeheartedly that you should only be embarrassed if you had something to hide. She, on the other hand, was perfect and was always happy to flaunt it. The world was her dressing room. That much had not changed.

❧

Scarlet was working feverishly as she stepped around her cluttered bedroom; piles of her weathered, worn, and otherwise "artfully destroyed" one-of-a-kind pieces of clothing were strewn everywhere. She'd decided it was time to cast off her old self, and she was making fast work of it to reduce the pain.

At first Scarlet had picked through her closets and drawers carefully, like a miner sifting for diamonds, but before long, she was grabbing armfuls of outfits that had once been precious to her and tossing them indiscriminately to the ground, prepping them for a trip to Goodwill. She could just about hear Petula walking by her open bedroom door and cracking yet again: "Is that your closet or a time machine?"

For a change, Scarlet felt, Petula might have a point.

"Sometimes vintage," Scarlet thought to herself, "is just old."

This was a realization that Scarlet had come by hard. She'd once crafted her outfits strictly for her own pleasure. The way she chose to dress had been a real act of pride, maybe even defiance. Not so much now, when everything she wore would turn up in knockoff versions on underclassmen a few days later, but not that long ago. She could remember being stared at, or worse, laughed at for her "look." Oddly, she missed that part of it. Much like having a personal assistant to prescreen potential friends, it had helped her to weed out the people she would never want to associate with. Besides, she felt that girls in velour tracksuits with chain store logos splashed across their asses had no right to say she looked bad.

What those girls, especially the ones who could afford to dress well, would never understand is that there is a big difference between having a sense of fashion and a sense of style. One comes from magazines, from what you're told; the other from your own imagination, what you feel, she thought as she added to the mound below her.

Revisiting all her old issues and foraging through her old clothes were becoming more and more commonplace for Scarlet these days. She wasn't sure if it was an early spring-cleaning bug she'd come down with, her pathological fear of boredom, or something much deeper. With school nearly over and Damen away at college, she had much too much time to think. And one of the things she had been thinking about quite a bit was Damen. She would have much preferred to be cleaning up for his visit, but he had exams and couldn't make it home for Valentine's Day.

Scarlet understood that school was a priority for him, but she was still a little upset about being alone. Not that she would ever show him. She wouldn't have minded going to see a midnight viewing of a V-Day slasher flick in 3-D, which happened to be their tradition. She felt just the slightest bit taken for granted. Would Petula, she thought, have ever stood for such treatment, or more the question, would he have even considered treating Petula this way in the first place?

She returned to the business at hand. Tossing all these things was like a little death for her. You might even call it murder, judging from the condition of her closets and the castoffs on the floor. But what was she trying to kill off, she wondered? Her past or her future?

As she stared down at the mounds of her once must-have apparel, she realized that in giving her stuff away, she was giving up her history, too—a history she'd shared, mentally, emotionally, and physically with Charlotte. Scarlet missed her terribly. Theirs was the most intimate relationship she'd ever had—at least so far. But even though she may have given herself over to Charlotte, she'd never given herself up, she thought, until now.

Chapter 4

Heart-Shaped Box

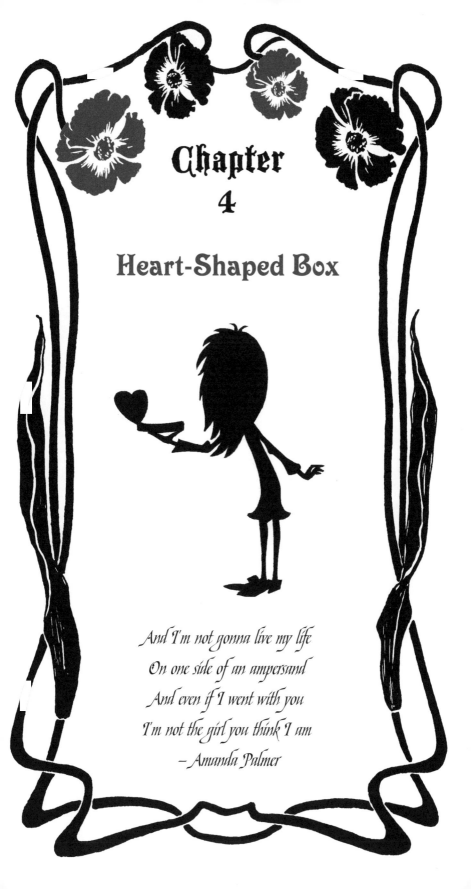

And I'm not gonna live my life
On one side of an ampersand
And even if I went with you
I'm not the girl you think I am
— Amanda Palmer

I against I.

We are often so distracted by the internal war between what we want to do and what we have to do that we overlook what we need to do. Not need in the sense of an obligation to others, but in the sense of a compulsion to preserve our own sanity. When doing what others think we should do comes into direct conflict with what our heads or hearts demand, it's time to choose whether our top priority is to please others or to please ourselves.

**etula strained to see through the** fogged-up windows of her brand-new BMW and down the darkened side street toward the glow emanating from the alley. As best she could determine, it was a garbage can spewing fire and smoke. The streetlamps were in disrepair and flickering, transforming the grimy scene from live-action into a stop-motion flip book.

After making sure the coast was clear, she hiked up the fur collar on her coal-black peacoat and stepped out of the car and onto the street, the loud clacking of her high heels against the cobblestones startling her for just a second.

"Shhhh," she hissed before realizing she was the only one there.

She reached back inside the car and grabbed the green plastic trash bag, which she'd been keeping in the trunk, from the passenger seat. Petula pulled down her sunglasses and stepped

lightly and quickly past the shuttered and steel-gated store-fronts, padlocked loading bays, broken pay phone, and grungy Dumpsters and tucked down an alleyway with the bale.

"Lock and load," Petula said, fixing her sights on the glowing target and the straggling crowd huddled around it.

Once she'd gotten close enough to catch a whiff of the unfortunates, she stopped and dug her heel tips into the crevice between cobblestones for stability. Petula then spun around a few times with the bag like a discus thrower, groaning out billows of cold breath into the night air, and let it fly. The sack landed and burst open like a watermelon dropped from a window ledge, spilling all kinds of high-end clothing, footwear, and accessories across the sidewalk. It looked like a fashion fireworks display gone awry.

Petula whirled back around on her heels and sprinted across the uneven surface for her car, her stealth mission accomplished. She pressed her automatic key to unlock the doors as she ran, and as the taillights blinked to acknowledge the command, they illuminated a car parked behind hers, sitting in total darkness. She couldn't make out a thing about it through her sunglasses, which being her disguise for the evening would be unthinkable to remove, and she was certain it wasn't there earlier.

It being the dead of night and all, Petula promptly freaked and sped toward the luxury sedan even faster. As she reached for the door handle, a loud, blaring voice called out, as if through a megaphone: "Stop right there."

Petula acted like she didn't hear—which was clearly impossible—and fumbled for the door handle, hoping whoever it was might take pity on her and just leave her alone.

"Don't move," the authoritative voice demanded, followed by a blaze of light that shot from a lantern on his car roof.

She could just make out the silhouette of a cop exiting his squad car through the glare of the floodlight.

"Thank God for oversize," she mumbled to herself, adjusted her sunglasses again, and raised her arms limply in a gesture of surrender.

She was discovered. Doing what, even *she* wasn't quite sure.

"Don't you know who I am?" Petula shouted frantically, flashing her ID in hopes of intimidating him. "I want to call my representatives."

"Turn around and place your hands on your vehicle, miss," the young officer, unimpressed, ordered calmly but firmly.

Petula felt the blood rushing to her face in embarrassment. She was busted. Exposed. What would her mom say? And Scarlet? Petula didn't even want to go there. Now The Wendys would find out all the details of her late-night excursions, which would confirm their worst suspicions, and possibly even give them an opening to overthrow her. *Et tu*, Wendy!

On the bright side, Petula pondered, she'd definitely take the best mug shot ever. She thought as fast as she could under the circumstances, hoping to distract the cop.

"Are they arresting people for wearing fur trim now?" Petula carped, turning her collar up and her head back around to look at him. "Or do you just want to frisk me?"

The patrolman remained silent and gave her a chance to settle down, which was definitely taking a while. He knew who she was. He'd graduated from Hawthorne a few years ahead of

her. But even without this background info, he wouldn't need to be a detective to see that a Hawthorne streetwalker couldn't afford the outfit she was wearing. He followed procedure nevertheless, pulled out his cuffs for effect, and asked her a few questions.

"What are you doing out here all alone at this time of night?" he asked. "This is a dangerous place for a young lady."

"I'm taking the Fifth," Petula rebuffed him, both unwilling and unable to explain. "I know my rights."

The officer just shook his head and stared at her. He'd only been on the force for a short while, but he was experienced enough to know he'd get nowhere with her.

"Take me to your leader," Petula uttered, confusing sci-fi with *CSI* as she extended her arms straight out in front of her and put her wrists together, offering herself up for arrest.

"This is just a warning, Miss Kensington," the officer said. "You're not under arrest, but I don't want to see you around here again."

"Really?" Petula said, her tough demeanor melting in relief. "Thank you, Officer, ahhh…"

Petula strained through her shades to read the name from his badge. No need to be so formal any longer, she figured; besides, he was kind of cute.

"Officer Beaumont," he proffered with a little smile. "Charlie Beaumont."

"Thank you, Charlie," Petula said gratefully, hanging her head ever so slightly.

"Stick with your blondetourage next time," Beaumont said, sarcastically referencing The Wendys, to indicate he

knew more about her than she would have thought. "There's strength in numbers."

"They're not blond," Petula corrected sheepishly, stroking her own locks. "They're just brunette with highlights."

Officer Beaumont walked away silently and returned to his vehicle to answer another call that was just coming across his police radio.

Petula got in her car and drove away slowly. Beaumont followed behind till she cleared downtown and then peeled off toward the next thruway exit. As she watched him turn away, she realized for the first time that night just how lucky she was that he was around.

Petula was never one to go out at night unaccompanied. Strength in numbers, but not for the reason Officer Beaumont cited. She needed to have her every decision supported, witnessed, and celebrated. It was kind of a like that whole "if a tree falls in a forest and no one hears it" thing. As a precautionary measure, Petula never set foot in a forest, thereby completely avoiding the possibility of falling alone.

What exactly did she think she was doing down there alone anyway? Dumping a bag of her used clothing on the street for a bunch of degenerates to pick through? Did she have some kind of death wish? Now *that* was an interesting bit of self-analysis.

Maybe she did. After all, this weird behavior pretty much dated back to her coma. She'd recovered physically, but she was not the same as before. She kept having all these thoughts — these feelings that were totally alien to her. She had become more observant of the world around her and far more aware of

and compassionate toward others and their troubles. Frankly, it was irritating.

Petula first started to notice her change of heart at Christmas. In the past, her time was spent window shopping and making notes about things she wanted, i.e., demanded, which she would then pass along to family and friends as a courtesy. She would even register on websites for their convenience, or to ensure that she got exactly what she requested in the right size. It was the season of giving, after all, and she liked to give her loved ones plenty of options.

But last Christmas, each time she visited the mall, the bells of the Salvation Army volunteers stationed at every door seemed to ring louder, until it was almost deafening to her. She found herself dropping pennies at first, then dimes, quarters, and even dollars into red kettles all over Hawthorne in a fruitless effort to make it stop. She was brought into painful conflict with values she'd held her whole life, and it was tearing her apart. For Petula, whose favorite motto was "Charity begins at home," preferably her home, giving to others was not an act of generosity; it was enabling.

But giving was at the core of both her erratic behavior and a growing philosophical dilemma. She prided herself on being part of "the problem," as others called it, rather than the solution, regarding those in need as losers who preferred to be victims rather than take control of their lives. Now, she was being compelled by an impulse she could neither understand nor control to help them.

But what could she do? There had to be more than secretly shot-putting bags of hand-me-downs to beggars.

She continued to grapple with this first-ever internal struggle of her life as she pulled into her driveway.

❧

Scarlet sat cozily on her bed drinking a double espresso and
wearing two oversize tanks—one was a flesh color and the
other was sort of a super-washed-out gray—layered on top of
one another and knotted on one side of the neck. They were
almost see-through and long enough to double as a minidress.
She had a cool vintage rhinestone brooch holding up the back
of her teased-out French twist, with only her ebony bangs
slightly curled under. Her lips were painted pale, a nude color,
and they were full and subtle. She looked like a modern Marie
Antoinette with edge.

Propped next to her was her guitar, which was covered in a
film of dust and looked like it hadn't been touched since she
and Damen last played together. All of the emotion she'd once
put into it lay silent. It just stood there, unwanted and abandoned, like some kind of relic of what she used to be.

She heard a car pull into the driveway and jumped off her
bed to peek out the window. Petula had a habit lately of walking through the side gate into the yard and coming in the
house from the back door. Sure enough, same routine. After a
minute, Scarlet heard the sliding glass door close, followed by
Petula's stomping footsteps.

As usual, her sister barged in without knocking, and in turn
received Scarlet's usual response: "Get out." Scarlet didn't even
bother to look up.

"Look what I found floating facedown in the pool," Petula

scolded, dangling Scarlet's dripping baby doll by its drenched Onesie.

"She needed a bath," Scarlet said, pushing the doll from her throw blanket so her bedding wouldn't get wet.

"Child abuser!" Petula barked. "This is negligence."

"How I raise Lil' bit is none of your business," Scarlet snapped dismissively. "Just because you color-coordinate with your little skinny-me doesn't mean you're going to pass."

"You are an unfit mother!"

"It's NOT a baby!" Scarlet yelled. "It's a stupid and sexist assignment. The boys don't have to do this crap."

Petula was a big believer in natural selection, but no longer applied the theory to kids and babies. Even fake ones. She had begun feeling an affinity for the downtrodden, especially orphans, ever since she'd noticed that most of the homeless people downtown were not much older than she and her sister were. Some were very much younger, abandoned and left to fend for themselves. Much like Scarlet's baby. Petula needed to act.

"I'd like to adopt your baby," Petula said with all sincerity.

"What?" Scarlet said, facing her in disbelief.

"That's right, I'll take her in," Petula continued. "Before you know it, you'll be selling her off to the highest bidder."

"Then maybe you should get your wallet," Scarlet said, trying to get rid of her. "And shut my door!"

Scarlet knew Petula well enough to assume that all she wanted two kids for was to upstage The Wendys or create a tabloid-worthy, celebrity-size brood. The dolls were accessories, not so different from a must-have nail color or skirt.

"I'll set up my room as a Safe Place, so you can drop the kid off anytime, no questions asked," Petula said.

Out of the corner of her eye, Scarlet noticed Petula scoping the piles of band tees, jeans, and cords that were strewn around the room.

"What were you doing out so late anyway?" Scarlet inquired.

"Let me help you," Petula offered, ignoring the question and instead scooping up an armload of her sister's castoffs.

"Don't trouble yourself," Scarlet responded insincerely.

"It's no trouble," Petula explained hesitatingly, as she picked up as much as she could carry. "I can cut up these old tees and make little rocker rompers. For, you know, the babies."

The fact that Petula would ask to borrow some of her seconds, even for a crafts project, was a clear sign to Scarlet that something was seriously wrong with her sister. But she decided not to show any concern and just play along.

"Suit yourself," Scarlet shot back skeptically, wondering what on earth had gotten into Petula now.

"Something like that," Petula answered cryptically.

Chapter 5

Playing the Angel

*But the thoughts we try to deny
Take a toll upon our lives
We struggle on in depths of pride
Tangled up in single minds
—Portishead*

Missed Oppurtunity.

———◆━✦━◆———

We don't miss what we never had, but we miss terribly things we almost had. And we miss things we used to have most of all. Though we hope and pray for our relationships, our looks, and our lives to improve, having more also means having more to lose.

he walk home after Markov's announcement—or sentencing, more appropriately—felt especially long today, which was fine with Charlotte. She was walking with Eric. They didn't get a lot of private time, so these strolls meant a lot to her, and to him, she hoped. She decided to take the opportunity to get to know him a little better, for Pam's and Prue's sake, if not for her own.

"So, where were you?" Charlotte asked.

"You mean when I was late for work this morning?" Eric asked.

"No, silly," Charlotte laughed. "Before you came *here*."

Eric tightened up a little. It was clear he didn't like talking about his past.

"I was a dropout," he volunteered slowly. "So even though I died onstage, I still had to go through Dead Ed to get my

boneyard GED, I guess," Eric said, the unpleasant memory of it obviously still with him.

"You were from Hawthorne, right?" Charlotte asked. "That's probably why they sent you here when you crossed."

"Could be," Eric said, sort of indifferently. "To be honest, I never really felt at home at Hawthorne."

"Neither did I," Charlotte added, noting something else they had in common.

Charlotte loved being with him. Not in a showy, PDA, look-at-me-I-have-a-boyfriend kind of way, but rather in a way that made her feel completely herself. Not at ease entirely, but comfortable. She felt she could tell him anything and he would understand. But she hadn't actually tried to until now.

"Do you think this new assignment is their way of keeping us apart?" Charlotte asked, hoping his reaction would provide the status of his feelings for her. It was the early days and she was still feeling pretty insecure.

"What's with all the conspiracy theories, Juliet?" Eric asked flatly. "That's not rock."

She still wasn't sure what actually constituted "rock" and what didn't, but she had come to understand that it was of the utmost importance to Eric. Not in a Metal Mike thickheaded way, she assured herself, but in the simple, cool, and charming Eric way.

Charlotte gulped, "I just mean, why now?" She pivoted, still looking for support, but a bit less obviously. "Aren't you suspicious at all?"

"Man, I thought it was rock stars that were supposed to have big egos," Eric responded, only half kidding.

Charlotte was hurt, and even Eric, who was not that great

at reading her moods, took her expression as a clear sign that he was being insensitive.

"I'm sorry, Charlotte," Eric said, brushing her arm with his, and almost, but not quite, grabbing for her hand. "But I don't see any conspiracy in this. It's just another thing we have to do to get where we need to go."

He was sounding a whole lot like her father, which was both comforting and irritating. Right about now, it was mostly irritating. Didn't he realize a break like this could spell death to a new relationship? To their relationship?

⊗◑

The Wendys were sharing a mini–rice cake outside the lunchroom and obsessing, as usual, about their waistlines and Petula.

"Did you see that Asian fusion brownie throwdown on the Food Network last night?" Wendy Anderson began. "Yum, yum."

"No, I was switching between the National Geographic Channel and Animal Planet last night," Wendy Thomas said. "I couldn't believe how fat all those natives are. Their stomachs are absolutely huge."

"It's all those carbs we send over!" Wendy Anderson concurred. "Somebody should airlift a few crates of Ab Rollers along with the rice and powdered milk."

"Simple substitutions like protein powder and brown rice," Wendy Thomas offered, "would do wonders."

"A little lean protein wouldn't hurt, and it's easy to get," Wendy Anderson said, "with all those animals running around."

They both needed a short break to savor and swallow the dried cracker.

"You know," Wendy Thomas mentioned, "it just occurred to me that, for most of the world, Animal Planet *is* the Food Network."

Just as Wendy Anderson was about to applaud her on that keen observation, Darcy sashayed up to them, interrupting their secret snackrifice to the Goal Weight Goddess. She was dressed expensively, but without a single logo blaring from her ass pocket or sleeve to blow her nouveau riche cover.

Both Wendys recoiled, pulling their heads back like threatened turtles. Darcy, The Wendys observed, had done her homework.

"You guys are The Wendys, right?" Darcy greeted. "Or is that just your circus name?"

"We don't have an act," Wendy Thomas shot back, clueless to the intended freak-show dis.

Darcy smirked, laughing to herself that the only thing these girls probably knew about Big Tops came from a plastic surgeon's office.

For their part, The Wendys were less offended than intrigued by the new girl's audacity.

"That's us," Wendy Anderson replied curiously, shushing Wendy Thomas. "And you are…?" Of course The Wendys knew but would never give Darcy the satisfaction of acknowledging it.

"Darcy," the girl answered, tilting her chin up slightly and sucking in her cheeks. "Your pleasure, I'm sure."

"What can we do for you?" Wendy Thomas asked regally.

"Sorry to disturb your *lunch*," Darcy quipped, noticing the rice cake, "but I had some information about Petula that I thought you might find interesting."

A total stranger gossiping about Petula? And using her name, no less? This was just not done. Much as the ancient Israelites were forbidden to speak the name of Yahweh, the students of Hawthorne refrained from talking about Petula in a familiar way.

The Wendys sheathed their claws momentarily because Darcy seemed to know something about Petula that they didn't know, a rare occurrence in WendyWorld.

"Go on," Wendy Thomas instructed tersely.

"I know someone who knows someone," Darcy said, speaking vaguely to protect her source, The Wendys assumed. "Who heard Petula got busted in an alley downtown last night."

"Doing?" Wendy Anderson asked, not wanting to seem out of the inner loop, but secretly dying to know.

"He didn't say," Darcy answered, "but I thought I should tell you first before it…you know, gets around the school."

Darcy knew that if such information ever leaked, The Wendys would be more than a little humiliated by association. With the end of senior year approaching, their legacies were at stake.

"How considerate of you," Wendy Thomas said flatly, her eyes squinting Darcy into even tighter focus.

"What do you want?" Wendy Anderson quizzed.

"Nothing," Darcy answered. "I just figured you guys have been embarrassed enough for two lifetimes."

"What do you mean?" Wendy Thomas asked.

"The whole coma thing, getting left back a year, and getting dumped by her boyfriend for her little sister," Darcy added snidely. "Now this."

She was making a blatant move against the Queen, a naked power play, and The Wendys were impressed. This was getting very political, and they were always up for a little intrigue. They still hadn't quite made up their minds, however, about what to make of this news or the messenger who delivered it.

"Let's just keep this confidential for now," Wendy Anderson urged, as she and Wendy Thomas flanked Darcy and walked her down the hall, out of the earshot of any curious bystanders.

Darcy was unfazed by their attempt to intimidate her.

"Consider it a gift," she said, strutting toward the exit and smiling as the third-period bell rang.

∞

The drama of the day continued when Charlotte arrived home, or rather she continued with the drama.

"What do you mean, you're going back?" Charlotte's mom asked, fighting back tears that would never come. "Bill?"

Her mom's outburst only served to feed the flame already burning in Charlotte's head. It felt good to be cared about so deeply. From her father's earnest countenance, she braced her-

self for the other side of the equation. He was a listener, rash neither in his words nor in his actions.

"It's not right," Charlotte complained out loud. "I have what I always wanted and now it's being taken away from me."

Charlotte was upset but also kind of excited. This was the first chance she'd ever had to vent to her parents. To be a child.

"Charlotte, we know how you're feeling. All we ever wanted was to be with you again, and now to find that you're leaving," Bill Usher began sympathetically. "But, you just may be needed for bigger things."

Charlotte was hoping for more than a feel-good speech. She wanted to be rescued from this predicament. She wanted to stay and he was being a…dad.

"Bill, this isn't right and you know it," Eileen said, the exasperation in her voice familiar to him.

"Eileen, look, what if your mother stopped you from moving to Hawthorne?" Bill offered rationally. "You never would have met me."

"No, but I'd be alive," Eileen said tersely.

Charlotte couldn't believe what had just slipped out of her mother's mouth, and neither could Eileen, from the expression on her face. It occurred to Charlotte that she wasn't the only one in her family who had carried unresolved issues over.

"This is so unfair," Charlotte said, echoing the sentiments of the zillions of whining teens before her, but more importantly, breaking the tension between her parents.

"It isn't very fair, but you need to see the big picture," Bill

said, the backlog of fatherly advice now just pouring from him. "You have a responsibility to yourself and your classmates, and you can't let them down."

Right now, Charlotte couldn't see the forest—only the trees. Especially the big giant one that looked like a totem pole with Markov's face carved into it and was blocking her path to ultimate happiness.

"Your father has a point. Even if we can't change the situation, we can change the way we look at it," Eileen said, embracing Charlotte with all her might, and heart.

Charlotte noted the reversal in her mother's tone and felt that Eileen had drawn some strength from her father's steadfastness. They were being a parental team, getting on the same page, and even though she disagreed, there was comfort and strength in their togetherness.

Eileen and Bill smiled, signaling to Charlotte that they were okay with it and that she would be okay, too. They hugged her tightly, squeezing the life out of her, so to speak.

Satisfied that the situation was under control, Bill gave her a peck on the cheek as he left the room. Eileen, however, was not as quick to call it quits.

"Charlotte, I know that you're upset about leaving us, even for a short while," her mom said, "but I get the feeling there is something else going on too."

Eileen saw right through Charlotte, and for once Charlotte was glad somebody could. Here it was, at last, and they both sensed it as only mothers and daughters can. It was what they'd waited for their whole lives and longer: for Eileen, a

chance to test-drive her "mother's intuition," and for Charlotte, a chance to have The Talk.

"Mom?" Charlotte stumbled as she searched for the right words to say.

"Yes, sweetie?" Eileen asked expectantly.

"There's this guy…," Charlotte began.

Chapter 6

You Can Do Better than Me

Love is a grave mental disease.
—Plato

Critical condition.

---◆◆◆◆◆---

Just as love blinds us to imperfections in others, it magnifies those we see in ourselves. But if this is true, then the opposite must also be the case. We can take comfort in the fact that our faults will be invisible to those who love us. The success or failure of any relationship depends not just on how we feel about each other, but on how we make each other feel about ourselves.

**harlotte, look at it this way: it's your**
first fight. That's the mark of a real relation-
ship," Pam said, trying to lift Charlotte's
spirits as they headed to the office for what was, for better or
worse, the last time.

This was not the time for "I told you so," though it took
every ounce of spectral strength from Pam and Prue not to
blurt it out.

"It just hurts me that he doesn't get that he's the main reason I want to stay," Charlotte said. "He's so casual about us."

"What 'us'?" CoCo butted in as she joined them on the
way. "Have you ever even talked about the both of you as a
couple?"

"No, not yet," Charlotte said.

"Maybe you're too afraid to find out what he really thinks,"
Prue added.

"I'd rather just vomit than be nauseated all day," CoCo said. "Know what I mean?"

They looked at CoCo, knowing there was a point, but unable to figure out what it was.

CoCo let out a sigh of exasperation and explained: "Just because you're afraid of what he might say, afraid of rejection, doesn't mean you just ignore it altogether. I would want to know."

"Let's not get too dramatic," Pam wisely advised.

"Maybe he thinks I'm not cool enough for him," Charlotte moped, her insecurities creeping back.

"He's a guy, Charlotte," Prue tossed off. "He's probably not thinking *anything*."

"And you are totally overthinking," Pam said. "This is the old you talking, Charlotte. Don't let yourself fall back into that trap."

Charlotte smiled a bit anxiously and realized they were probably right.

"At least he's getting sent back with us so you can keep your eye on him," Pam pointed out rationally.

"Yeah," CoCo tweaked. "Leaving him behind could be dangerous now that Polly is here."

"Thanks a lot," Charlotte grumbled. "I feel *much* better now."

Pam and Prue laughed good-naturedly and nudged Charlotte as they approached the phone bank. Charlotte didn't see the humor in any of it just then. Just the injustice.

ॐ

"Why so glum, man?" Mike prodded Eric, who seemed uncharacteristically stuck in a funk. "I thought you were looking forward to getting back."

"I am," Eric said weakly. "It's just, you know, Charlotte's kind of bumming me."

"Don't *fret*," DJ chided, proud of his guitar pun. "This is not like you."

"I don't know," Eric said. "This trip is really bad timing for us."

"It's perfect timing!" Mike shouted, punching out an air-drum roll in front of him. "You don't want to be tied down with all that living tail that's gonna be around."

"Brodown!" DJ shouted, anticipating his first boys' night out in quite some time.

Subtlety was definitely not a priority for this crew, but judging from the look on Eric's face, they could tell they might have gone a little too far.

"Aw, she'll be cool," DJ assured him, reeling the conversation back. "She's got plenty to keep her busy."

"What do you mean?" Eric asked, taken aback.

"Damen," Mike explained indelicately. "He's the whole reason she's here."

"She died trying to hook up with him," DJ continued. "Good thing too, or we'd all still be *there*."

"Yeah, good thing," Eric mumbled.

❧

The entire office staff arrived on time for a change. All were anxious to hear from Markov. All except for Charlotte, that is.

She snuck a nervous peek at Eric, as she usually did, and he nodded back and smiled, which she hoped was a good sign.

A not-so-good sign was that her Dead Ed teacher Mr. Brain wasn't there. His presence was always comforting, especially for Charlotte, but his absence was not exactly surprising. After all, his most recent graduates had just arrived on campus, and he really only showed up for super-special occasions now.

Charlotte figured this return engagement that Markov had booked for them probably didn't qualify. They'd been told they were going back, but not much else. It was all very mysterious, and the tension in the room was palpable.

"Today," Markov began, "is the first day of the rest of your afterlives."

The audible groan from the Eric-Mike-DJ section in the back was contagious and, not surprisingly, Markov quickly began to lose the room. He sounded like a personality-challenged straight-A student giving a hackneyed valedictory address. Bor-ing.

"That's original," Eric, who had set himself up as a bit of a nemesis to Markov, opined sarcastically.

"Yeah," Charlotte continued. "Should we remember to always reach for the stars and follow our dreams too?"

Chuckles rolled through the room, but not from Pam and Prue, who found the back talk irresponsible and really out of character for Charlotte. Eric was always a bit of a class clown, but for Charlotte, this was virgin territory.

"Trying to impress the boyfriend?" Pam chided Charlotte dryly.

"*That's* original," Prue concurred. "What a rebel."

Given the divisive mood in the room, it was clear that Markov was not the best person to deliver this message, but he was not easily deterred. He not only commanded their attention, he demanded it. Markov took all this very seriously, and after a false start, the interns began to as well.

"I have a question," Call Me Kim announced, thrusting her arm up, before Markov could utter another word. "Are we being promoted or fired?"

Kim had been an A student in life, a team player in Dead Ed, and an exemplary employee at the phone bank. As a firm advocate of the merit system, she could not imagine being replaced on a whim. So maybe it was neither. Maybe this was what the end was: obsolescence. The new kids had arrived to man the phones, and they were no longer needed.

"I know you are all a little confused," Markov offered.

"That's like saying Silent Violet is a little quiet," Charlotte huffed.

"Don't drag me into this," Violet demurred, seeking to remain neutral.

"Change is a part of life," Markov said. "Of learning, of growth."

"And death?" Charlotte queried, frustrated. "You don't grow after you're dead?"

"Not true," CoCo interjected, peeking out from her Hermes scarf. "Your hair and nails do."

"Coooooool," Metal Mike droned, imagining his hairy,

jagged-toed corpse busy transforming into a human can opener in its casket.

"But what if you're all changed already?" Charlotte pressed. "What do we get then? Just to…rest in peace?"

"Don't you know the answer to that question by now, Charlotte?" Markov continued. "Resting in peace is a fantasy created to placate the living." He paused. "Not the dead."

"It's just that there was finally time," Charlotte mumbled, glancing at Eric. "Time to do the last things we wanted to do."

"Don't worry, Charlotte," Markov chided. "You'll live."

Charlotte didn't find his little joke funny in the least, and he realized that immediately.

"You completed your internship and now, now it's time for a little on-the-job training," he added.

"Think of it as a working vacation," CoCo soothed, offering a unique take on things. "Sort of an executive perk, like walking the Dior showroom after hours."

"Or the plumbing supplies aisle at Home Depot," Bud added, keeping it real.

"Or crashing an after-hours house party," DJ beamed. "Uninvited."

"We get to go back, knowing what we know now…," Violet said, unusually chatty.

"There's nothing to stop us," twins Simon and Simone said in unison.

Charlotte was all alone now in her convictions. Even Pam, her B.D.F.—Best Dead Friend—had flipped on her.

Markov was determined to get things back on track.

"Well, sorry to disappoint you all, but it's not going to be a dead-kids-gone-wild kind of thing," Markov instructed. "You're each going to have an assignment."

"What now?" Charlotte relented, asking on behalf of the assembly.

"As I already told you," Markov informed, "you are going back."

"Back where?" DJ asked.

"To where you came from," Markov said. "Hawthorne."

Charlotte suddenly perked up. Back to Hawthorne meant back to Scarlet.

"Why there?" Eric asked, disappointed. "Couldn't we go someplace, you know, cooler?"

He was hoping for a bigger pond to swim in. One where he might be able to showcase his mad guitar skills at last and just maybe get a taste of the fame that escaped him.

"Start small and work your way up," Markov advised, talking as much about Hawthorne as about Eric's "career."

"I don't need a dress rehearsal," Eric gruffed.

"This isn't a debate society or a democracy," Markov snapped, his expression darkening. "You are being sent where you are needed."

"I don't get it," Kim persisted. "To do what, exactly?"

"Whatever is necessary," Markov said simply, perusing the list he had been holding. "You'll just have to figure it out."

Charlotte was alarmed immediately. If they were going back, something must be wrong. All reservations about returning melted away. She put on her game face.

"You were right," Eric mouthed to Charlotte, no longer so anxious to get back. "This is bogus."

Charlotte didn't react at all. She seemed focused, motivated. He had never seen her like this. And he wasn't sure how he felt about her eagerness to return all of sudden, given the gossip from Mike and DJ about her ex.

"Listen up, people," Markov barked. "Here are your assignments."

"Is this some kind of test?" Suzy asked, nervously picking away at her phantom forearm scars for the first time that she could remember.

"That's one way to think of it," Markov said brusquely. "I prefer to call it a mission."

"Mission?" Charlotte asked. "What kind of mission?"

"Your mission is to help the living deal with their problems," Markov detailed, ignoring the interruption. "Not to solve big issues like war and peace, but rather the petty problems that plague their lives and consciences—the little things that paralyze them and sometimes stop them from living."

"Little things?" Charlotte asked, hoping for some clarification.

"There is nothing bigger," Markov answered.

"Wait, so we're the ones who are dead," Eric said, "and we're supposed to help these living losers see how good they have it?"

"Right," Markov said. "It's what you've been preparing for here."

"But we're not experts," Charlotte complained. "Who will help us help them?"

"The new class will be here as your lifeline," Markov assured them. "So will I."

It was a surprisingly supportive statement from Markov, and they knew he was a man of his word.

"So, we're sponsors?" Prue asked. "Like in some kind of supernatural intervention?"

"Sounds more like spiritual guides to me," Pam added.

"Like angels," Charlotte said succinctly.

"Technically, yes," Markov said. "But not in the white toga, wings, and halo sense."

"Thank God," CoCo added. "Halos are a hair-don't."

The interns stared ahead wide-eyed as Markov scanned down his list, pairing each with what seemed to be a random counterpart at Hawthorne. Mike, DJ, Suzy, Abigail, Jerry, Bud, Simon, Simone, Violet, and Kim each left to say their farewells to family as their names were called and assignment given.

"CoCo," Markov continued. "Your pairing is with…Petula Kensington."

Wow, Charlotte thought to herself. Not so long ago she would have been so jealous for anyone but her to get Petula.

"Ciao!" CoCo gave a quick wave, grabbed her purse, and split.

"Pam," Markov went on, "Wendy Anderson is all yours."

"Lucky you," Prue laughed.

"Prue," Markov announced. "You've got Wendy Thomas."

Prue almost choked on her own tongue as Pam had the last laugh. They both made devil horns on their heads and departed.

"With all the problems in the world?" Charlotte pleaded skeptically. "There's got to be something more important for us to do than go back to help some spoiled rotten high school kids with their relationship issues."

"No," Markov answered definitively. "There really isn't."

Charlotte and Eric were the only two left in the room. They felt like the final two contestants on some hidden-camera game show. Charlotte sort of felt like the fix was in, however, because she knew what was coming next. She'd get Scarlet and Eric would get Damen. How weird, she thought, but at least she'd finally get to introduce Eric to two of the most important people in her past.

"Charlotte," Markov read. "Your partner will be…"

"Yes," she chirped expectantly, clapping her hands in excitement.

"Damen Dylan."

Charlotte was stunned. Once upon a time, she would have fainted at such news. But now? What could possibly be the point of all this? Eric misread the look of amazement on her face and felt an unfamiliar emotion take hold of him: jealousy.

"Isn't he the reason you're here?" Eric prodded. "The love of your life?"

Charlotte still couldn't speak. There was still one person left to be assigned.

"Eric," Markov concluded. "You've got…"

"Scarlet Kensington," Charlotte mouthed along with Markov.

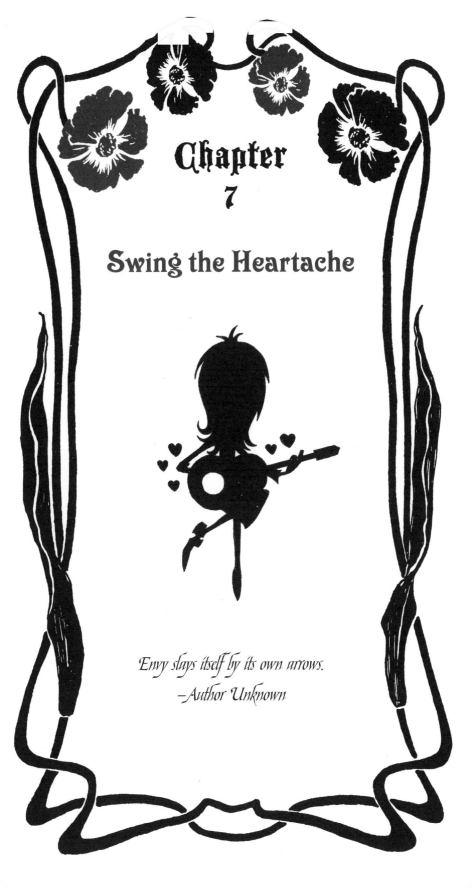

Chapter 7

Swing the Heartache

Envy slays itself by its own arrows.
–Author Unknown

Lovesick.

Rather than heal us, love can also harm, unleashing a pandemic of debilitating emotions that transform us into a person we barley recognize and cost us that which we so desperately desire. Sudden outbreaks of insecurity, jealousy, obsession, or just plain fear can be contributing factors in our heartache. And though the symptoms of lovesickness may be many, they all share a single cause and single cure: You.

alentine's Day started like any other day at the Kensington house, other than the foul moods it tended to generate. The only real difference was that the newspaper resting on the stoop outside was barely visible, covered by the flowers, candy, and balloons left on the bluestone steps by not-so-secret admirers. It was an annual ritual that Petula had come to expect as much as the Thanksgiving Day parade.

Actually, it was more a memorial. All Petula's admirers knew that she would stab them in the heart without batting a Colossal lash and would normally just kick everything off on her way to school, but today, she was a little bit more touched.

"Hey, baby-killer, go see if there are any dark chocolate caramels out there," Petula yelled from her room. "Nothing less than seventy-two percent cocoa, please."

"I don't have time to work out antioxidant content right

now," Scarlet yelled back. "I'd spell it out for you but I don't have any crayons with me."

"A little tense, are we?" Petula chided as she glided down the stairs. "Maybe you should chow down on a piece of that dark chocolate and get your blood pressure in check."

"Thank you, Doctor Google," Scarlet snarked. "You are a regular search engine scholar."

"I'm just trying to be helpful," Petula said. "You don't want to turn your pretty pale face red before Damen gets back."

"He's not coming home," Scarlet said, trying to play it off.

"Ouch," Petula consoled, barely masking her glee. "Absence makes the heart grow fungus, I guess."

Petula picked up Scarlet's baby and began talking to it in her trademark passive-aggressive way.

"I know she appears to be heartless," she said to the baby. "But don't worry: I'm sure she has four or five backup hearts in the freezer."

Classic Petula, Scarlet thought, going right for the jugular like that. For every flicker of compassion she occasionally showed these days, she could still flame-broil you with cruelty. The frosty relationship between them had thawed somewhat since "the coma," but lately Petula just seemed more distant than ever. Scarlet figured they were like strangers who clutched each other tightly during a rough flight but returned to business as usual once the pilot regained control and the plane landed safely.

"Hate you," Scarlet called out sweetly as Petula made her way out the front door.

"Hate you too," came the sugary reply.

Much like Scarlet's wardrobe, her decor was evolving too. Long gone, courtesy of a wet sponge and sharp straightedge razor blade, were the band bumper stickers that had transformed her bathroom into a museum-quality reproduction of a stall at a punk club. They had been replaced by strings of exposed lightbulbs hanging from the vanity in bunched bouquets. It was her modern interpretation of a 1920s chandelier.

Her bedroom looked like an old Hollywood boudoir, kind of art nouveau with an eccentric twist. She even had a real vanity with all kinds of jewelry, compacts, perfume bottles, and powders. She still had all the rare indie movie posters hanging in her room, but now they were displayed in ornate gold frames. It was that way with her too. She was the same, just kind of framed differently.

Scarlet started picking up stuff off the floor and straightening up her bed. She wanted her room to look perfect for her V-Day cyber chat with Damen, and she hadn't gotten around to bagging her things up and dropping them off yet. Petula had helped de-bulk the pile some, but for whatever reason, Scarlet just could not bring herself to part with the rest.

She soon found herself rummaging through the remainder of the heap. She could have opened a vintage shop with all the stuff she had, but those outfits were so personal to her, so much a part of her past, her identity. She would rather toss them than sell them.

She could still smell the memories in them, put them on

and be there, back in the moment. She wasn't the sentimental type, by any means, but she found herself missing the old Scarlet, even envying the self that existed before she fell in love. Love did change you, that much was true, she conceded, but not as much as you change yourself.

The whole idea of transforming into someone or something else was all starting to get to her, so she decided to go for a little walk to clear her head. She wandered around town, stopping at IdentiTea for a free drink — courtesy of her employee discount — then to some little vintage stores and record shops she and Damen used to hit on Saturday afternoons.

Around the corner, she poked her head into Split, the all-ages club where she'd see new bands. It had changed ownership and decor a few times in the past few years, but the kids were still coming to hear acts they couldn't see anywhere else. In fact, there was one band loading in for sound check, so she stuck around to watch them set up.

After a couple of minutes, she noticed someone standing up against the wall checking out the stage and occasionally looking in her direction, as well. He seemed to hide in the shadows thrown by the light rig installed above the stage. He didn't appear to be with the crew or the band, but he sure looked like he could have been. From what she could see, which wasn't much, he definitely had the indie-boy look down cold.

Up close, things became much clearer. She was surprised to see that he was wearing a Dead Boys tee, just like one she had given away. In fact, everything he had on was totally authentic — no cheaply made reproductions that she could

spot—and would definitely have cost a fortune at the local vintage boutiques, if you were lucky enough to even find this stuff. The most striking thing about it all was that he didn't sport his kit pretentiously, like a rock-and-roll costume. He wore it naturally, comfortably, like, well, clothing.

She always thought she would end up with a guy who looked like he did: tall and built, but skinny; coal-black dyed hair and pale skin; and the attitude to go with it. He looked like the kind of guy who had groupies, but didn't care because all that mattered to him was being onstage, performing. He was intimidating, even at first glance.

"Cool band," Scarlet blurted, pointing to his T-shirt.

There was no response. He just kept staring at the stage, nodding along to the beat the drummer was laying down. The low-tech P.A. system, which was buzzing like crazy, wasn't very chat-friendly, she thought. She waited until it quieted down and tried again.

"Love their live album," she called out again, hoping to strike up a conversation. "*Liver Than You'll Ever Be*?" She paused for a response that didn't come. "*Night of the Living Dead Boys* is probably my favorite, though."

Still nothing.

"Hey," Scarlet moved in closer and yelled snidely above the din. Like Petula, she was not accustomed to being ignored.

"You talking to me?" the guy asked with a confused look on his face, like she was begging for money or something.

Scarlet didn't mind a little attitude, but rudeness was a different thing altogether.

"You see anybody else here?" Scarlet said, spinning her head around.

"Sorry. I'm Eric," he responded, his expression softening.

"Scarlet," she said. "You from around here?"

"Yeah, I used to, ah...," Eric stammered briefly, unsure of how to respond, "live here."

"Cool tee. I have, or should I say had, one myself," she continued. "You find yours at Clothes Minded?"

"Nah," he said, completely oblivious to the whole idea of a vintage store.

Scarlet didn't press, figuring he didn't want to give away any fashion secrets to a nosy stranger.

"Are you with these guys?" she asked, changing the subject.

"No," Eric said again. "I got my own thing."

"Do you play?"

"Guitar," Eric said. "And I write a little."

Suddenly a surly voice blasted out of the speakers and filled the club.

"This is a closed sound check," the roadie barked. "Out!"

"Well, I guess I'll see you around," Scarlet said. "Eric, right?"

"Looks like you will," he added vaguely, handing her a cassette. "Here's a demo tape of my stuff. Let me know what you think."

She was flattered that he would share his music with her, but the audiotape thing threw her. She hadn't even seen one of those since her easy-to-use Playskool tape deck broke. She figured he was into a retro vibe though, considering his look, which, being a vintage fan herself, was just fine with her.

Scarlet was multitasking manically, cleaning and streaming, as she fired up the laptop for her iDate with Damen. He liked to joke that he was just a double click away, but cyberspace was no substitute for personal space, as far as she was concerned. Still, it was all Valentine's Day was going to be this year, and she was determined to make the best of it. As the muted ring turned to a shrill drone, she knew connection was at hand. When they were both logged on, Scarlet kissed the screen to start the session. Damen was watching her every move, even though he was supposed to be cramming.

"I'm so sorry I couldn't be there tonight," Damen offered. "Good thing you hate Valentine's Day."

"Yeah," Scarlet said halfheartedly. "Good thing for you."

"You're okay with it, right?" Damen asked rhetorically, since the choice was moot anyhow.

"Aren't you supposed to be studying?" she reminded him, changing the subject as she bent over to pick up a pile of clothes.

"Oh, I am," Damen replied, eyeing her backside.

Just then an announcement came over the radio about a songwriting contest.

"You should enter."

"Can't…it's Shark Week," Scarlet said, trying to blow it off.

"You really should," Damen prodded. "You could win."

"I could also sell my kidney for cash," Scarlet snarked, "but you don't see me doing that, do you?"

And to Scarlet they would have felt about the same since both possibilities involved turning her insides out for the world to see. Invasive and painful. Besides, she didn't really feel competent enough as a writer or a musician to submit a song in a real competition. Drawing adoring crowds at IdentiTea was one thing, but assaulting the public airwaves, even the local ones, was quite another. She logged off the station and pressed Play on her cassette deck, putting Eric's music center stage.

Scarlet plucked out a tee from her big pile, getting back to her cleanup.

"Hey! I remember that," Damen said, pointing to the tee that Scarlet had on for their first tutoring session. "What are you doing with it?"

"Giving it away," Scarlet sighed sentimentally, as she tossed it onto an enormous pile outside her door. "Just doesn't feel like me anymore."

"Yeah, it's not really you anymore."

It was okay for Scarlet to admit to that, but she secretly resented that fact that Damen was so quick to agree. Their Valentine's date had definitely not gotten off to the kind of start either of them was hoping for.

"Hey, what's that?" Damen asked as she pulled back.

Scarlet freaked for a second and thought the videocam might have magnified the tiny blemish on her chin. Another very un-Scarlet moment, she thought to herself.

"What's what?"

"The music," Damen clarified.

"Oh, that. It's just from a sampler someone gave me," Scar-

let said, having forgotten the tunes she'd left blaring in the background.

"Who gave it to you?" he asked pointedly.

He sounded a little jealous, even though he was not the jealous type. Music was a very personal thing between them, and she always shared everything new she had with him. From his tone, she thought he was a little perturbed that she'd forgotten to mention it but had obviously thought enough of it to leave it playing during their chat. She liked that he cared.

"Some guy," Scarlet said casually. "It was a tape, if you can believe it."

"Is it any good?" Damen probed, already thinking it was, based on what he could hear through the tiny speakers on his computer.

"I haven't really listened yet," Scarlet said casually. "I have to digitize it. Right now, I'm playing it on an old Hello Kitty tape deck I found in the attic."

"The attic?" Damen chided. "You went to a lot of trouble."

If she were being honest, she kind of did. She was dying to hear it, even though she wasn't sure why.

"I knew where it was," Scarlet said a little defensively.

"Well, what else have you been listening to lately?" Damen asked.

"Nothing special," Scarlet said. "I've just been streaming stuff online, mostly."

"What about your iPod?" Damen pressed.

"Honestly, I can't even find it," Scarlet said, beginning to get a little impatient with all this music talk. "My earbuds are broken anyway."

"They're probably under your pillow or something," Damen responded. "Why don't you check?"

Scarlet thought it was a pointless suggestion, but her room was so topsy-turvy it could be anywhere. She decided to humor him. As she searched around under the supersized crushed velvet bolster, she felt what seemed to be a small box. She took it out from underneath the pillow and saw it was wrapped simply in brown paper but adorned with a tiny bunch of micro-mini Peter Pans. It was beautiful.

"What is this?" she asked, completely stunned.

She opened the box and pulled out her old iPod.

"Turn it on," he demanded.

"That's your job," Scarlet said sarcastically.

She booted up the player and reached for the earbuds underneath and pulled out brand-new ones. They were earbuds in the shape of hearts. A note at the bottom of the box said, "Y.T.N.F."

He had to have someone on the inside, and she knew pretty much who that person was. In fact, Scarlet was almost touched by it. Petula had never done anything kind for her or for anyone else before. This was a first. It also explained, Scarlet thought, all that poking around her room her sister had been doing lately.

"Go on, listen," he said.

As she selected the playlist, tears started streaming down her face, and her hazel eyes got brighter and glassier and even more piercing. Damen had loaded the player with all their favorite songs—songs that told their story, songs that meant something. Scarlet stared at the tiny roses and began to won-

der if Damen's message was not just in the music, but in the Peter Pans as well. Then again, maybe she was reading too much into it. He definitely meant for the gift to show her how he felt, though.

"I love it," Scarlet said as Damen sat there anxiously waiting for her reaction. "I love you," she added softly.

"You do?" Damen asked proudly.

"Damen, don't you know?" Scarlet asked. "Can't you see the writing on the wall?"

Damen wasn't following.

"The writing on the wall, can't you see it?" Scarlet asked again, pointing her finger at the computer screen and directing him to look over his shoulder. Damen turned around, but all he could see was the "This Is Not a Love Song" promo PiL poster that she'd given him hanging on the wall over his bed.

"Take the poster down," she said.

He gently removed the tape from the top of the panoramic poster that practically filled up his whole wall, careful not to tear it, and peeled it off, revealing line after line of song lyrics written largely in Scarlet's handwriting across the room. He was stunned.

"I wrote it for you," Scarlet said sweetly, smiling.

"How did you do this?" Damen wondered aloud.

"I sent your roommate a scan from my song diary," Scarlet explained. "He printed it off on clear vellum sheet and put it in an art projector and enlarged it. He traced it to look like my handwriting."

It was breathtaking, magical, and unbelievably romantic.

"I can't believe you did this," Damen said.

"I thought it would ward off any female stragglers that happened to find their way into your dorm room."

"You are amazing," he said.

He put his hand to the screen, and she to hers, as they logged off for the night.

Damen lay with his head at the foot of the bed for a long while, strumming his guitar, reading and rereading the words of Scarlet's song, and deciphering the layers of meaning as only he could.

Scarlet transferred the audiotape to her computer and loaded the converted MP3 files into her refurbished player. She listened to Eric's demo playing through her new earbuds from Damen as she drifted off to sleep.

☙❧

The Wendys staked out the Kensington house from the backseat of Wendy Anderson's car and waited for Petula to make a move. They were sporting Double Agent chic, donning cream-colored silk kerchiefs and sunglasses to make themselves look not only deep, but fashionably undercover. They justified their spying by pretending that an intervention was in Petula's best interest, not just theirs.

As hoped, Petula strolled out into the cold night air dragging a full-to-bursting black heavy-duty contractor's bag she'd "borrowed" from the landscapers. She lifted it into the passenger seat of her Beemer and took off. The Wendys tailed Petula all the way downtown in the freezing cold. It was rare for them to be down there to begin with, but totally unheard of after dark. Petula had slowed down and pulled

around the corner just ahead. They could see the glare from her brake lights around the bend and figured she must have stopped.

"Where are we?" Wendy Anderson asked her copilot.

Hawthorne was a small place with an even smaller downtown, but their inexperience with the seedy neighborhood required research. Wendy Thomas studied the dashboard GPS and pinpointed their location.

"Um," Wendy Thomas replied not-so-confidently, "downtown?"

"What is she doing down here?" Wendy Anderson asked.

Before Wendy Thomas could respond, the taillights on Petula's car dimmed and then went black. They heard her car door pop open and quickly slid down as low in their seats as possible, leaving only their head wraps visible above the dashboard. Petula walked around the corner, head down, her shadow cast by the streetlights, growing ever longer the farther away from them she walked.

"Do you think she saw us?" Wendy Anderson queried nervously.

"Shut up, Wendy," Wendy Thomas commanded. "You're fogging the windows and I can't see a thing."

It wasn't Wendy Anderson's big mouth that was causing the windows to cloud over, however, but rather the cool presence of Pam and Prue, who'd just crashed The Wendys' Emma Peel party. They settled in the backseat and immediately began tracing rude messages onto the glass.

Each time Wendy Anderson wiped away the condensation, Wendy Thomas's breath would reveal a new insult on

the windshield: "Hoe-tards," "fugly," "shallowficial." The looks on their faces were priceless, and Pam and Prue could barely contain themselves.

"This is going to be great," Prue laughed. "Who needs heaven?"

Pam smiled and nodded but quickly straightened up when she caught a glimpse of Petula stopping and standing on a barren corner, as if she was keeping an appointment. She pointed Prue in her direction, as The Wendys, oblivious to their guests, followed.

"You don't think...," Wendy Anderson let the thought that Petula might be involved in some kind of secret affair, or worse, hang in the air.

For just a second, The Wendys' hard-heartedness seemed to soften, and they looked at each other with almost genuine concern for their leader. The moment was fleeting, however, as they quickly allowed all kinds of alternative theories to fill their small minds.

"Maybe she's a serial killer," Wendy Anderson offered.

"That would explain a lot," Wendy Thomas concurred.

"It really would," Prue grumbled, as Pam just shook her head dismissively.

The passengers, dead and alive, remained fixated on Petula, as a solitary figure in tattered clothing approached her from the dark end of the street. Petula stood nervously and then began chatting with the bag lady, or rather bag girl. They were all speechless until Wendy Thomas shrieked.

"Oh my God," Wendy Thomas yelled. "The smoking gun."

She tried documenting the whole sordid transaction with her phone camera, but the broken streetlamps seemed to cut out on cue and come to Petula's defense. All she got was a black screen. So, she and Wendy Anderson were left to just observe as Petula handed over item after item of clothing.

"She's, like, a missionary," Wendy Anderson surmised.

"I think that toe thing really did go to her brain," Wendy Thomas suggested, prompting nods of agreement from Pam and Prue. "She's insane."

"Darcy was right," Wendy Thomas said, staring in disdain and disbelief at the scene unfolding in front of her. "Time for a friendectomy."

Chapter 8

Pictures of You

Send me the pillow
The one that you dream on.
—The Smiths

I second that emulsion.

Sometimes it's the things that are all around us that are hardest to see, especially love. Like dust particles suspended in a ray of sunshine, love remains invisible to us until it is illuminated. When our hearts can't see clearly, love creates a Tyndall effect of its own, helping us to shine a light on what is always there, even in our darkest times.

**harlotte found herself on a sidewalk** in front of an industrial-looking building. It could have been an office tower, an apartment building, or a prison, from the looks of it, and if she didn't know better, she would have sworn she was still on the afterlife compound. There were huge differences here, however, like traffic, leafy trees, lawns, and people. Lots of young people. And a sign that said "State College."

The building in front of her was where she belonged — where Damen belonged. She walked through the double glass doors and into the lobby, where she noticed a register of students and room assignments. Charlotte picked out Damen's name right away, as if it was highlighted, and tried to ignore the crush of kids passing around and through her on their way to class, or on their way to skip class.

Charlotte waited at the elevator for someone to push the

Up button and rode up to his floor, just to get the hang of it all again. It hadn't been all that long since her trip back to rescue Petula, but she was rusty. It was definitely taking her a minute to get her "life legs" under her. When the doors opened, Charlotte walked down the gray indoor/outdoor carpeted hallway to Damen's room and literally poked her head through his door, looking for signs of life. No one was around, which was just as well. She needed a minute to gather herself. Charlotte walked over to the window and looked down onto the square.

She looked around Damen's room and headed for his desk. There were some textbooks piled up on the floor, a few trophies, a guitar and amp, two unmade twin-size beds, a ratty couch, stained coffee table, and of course, some state-of-the-art electronics — a black surround-sound speaker system that dangled from the beige walls, a DVD player, a silver-edged flat-screen TV, and the latest computer and all the peripheral toys to go with it.

This was a guy's room all right, not really that different from Damen's room back home, as she recalled from her single visit there. Apart from a poster or two the only color in the room was a few pictures she noticed above his desk, thumbtacked to his cork bulletin board. She leaned in closer to get a better look.

"What's he doing with pictures of another girl?" Charlotte thought as she studied the photo.

She gasped when she realized it wasn't a stranger at all, but Scarlet. The girl in the picture was styled and groomed so perfectly, looked so grown-up.

As she turned from the desk, the next thing that caught her eye was Damen's unmade bed and the unexpected writing on the wall above it. Charlotte walked over to it, studying every slant, tracing each stroke like an amateur graphologist. It was Scarlet's—there was no mistaking it—and the sentiment was beautiful, but Charlotte could see trouble in it too. Something was wrong.

Charlotte returned to the picture and took an even closer look. It was definitely from a recent event, New Year's Eve, maybe. Damen was smiling, Scarlet too, but the way he was holding her so tightly, and the way she was leaning away, ever so slightly, spoke volumes. Still, Charlotte checked herself; maybe she was looking for problems where there weren't any. An unfortunate side effect of her reverse commute to reality.

"Welcome back," Charlotte said to herself. "To the same old stuff."

She sat down on the couch and waited for Damen to arrive.

☜☞

Scarlet slept in stereo, having nodded off to Eric's demo tape blaring from her new heart-shaped earbuds. It was late when she awoke, and she rushed to grab a shower and get dressed. Dressing, she found, was an unusually difficult chore for her today.

With nothing for her to wear coming to mind, the ever-shrinking pile of potential discards on her floor caught her eye. She picked up a black, oversize off-the-shoulder sweatshirt she used to love and turned it back to front a few times.

She remembered just about everything she'd ever done in it. The more she looked at it, the more she realized that she still loved it. She threw it on over some dark, iridescent leggings, and wore it as a cool minidress.

The whole issue of what to wear should not have been such a big deal, because Scarlet didn't have anything major planned, just some errands. But she would be passing by Split along the way, and she just never knew who she might run into there.

On her way out the door, she stopped in the kitchen and grabbed the set of keys to her old car, which had been sitting in the driveway with a "For Sale" sign in the rear window since Thanksgiving. At first, Petula put it there as a prank—she hated the car so much—but after a while Scarlet decided to sell it. It just wasn't her anymore either, as Damen had so incisively or insensitively—she still wasn't quite sure—noted about her wardrobe. She'd been driving around her mom's Jetta ever since.

Scarlet pulled open the heavy driver's side door, got into the black jalopy, and dug herself into the cracked and worn leather upholstery. She pumped the gas pedal a few times; turned the ignition, prompting a couple of coughs from the tailpipe; cranked up her stereo; and then hurried on her way.

After hitting the dry cleaner's and a few vinyl shops, Scarlet found herself near the club. She drove up and parked right in front, making sure the car would be completely visible to anyone inside.

Another load-in was in progress for another band, and as Scarlet poked her head in, she had very low expectations that Eric would be hanging out. She looked around, and there he

was, same as the day before, watching the stage like he'd never left.

"Hey," she called out as she walked over. "I listened to your tape."

She didn't tell him what she thought of it right away; it wasn't like Scarlet to give too much. She wasn't sure what she was reading on his face, but it definitely wasn't surprise. He almost seemed to be expecting her.

"You came all the way down here to tell me that?" he asked.

"That," she said flatly, "and that your drummer could use a metronome."

He laughed a little, knowing she was definitely right about that, but when it came to punk music, sloppy beats were a sign of cred, of rawness. The best music, she always felt, was about emotion and energy, not so much about structure, precision, or even ability. She prided herself on making her own music in that way, and she definitely heard a lot of it in Eric's.

"So, you're into timing?" he said with a wink, but not the cheesy kind. It was kind of cool and flirty.

"Don't you want to know what I thought about the tape?" she asked, playing it up a little.

"Well, seeing that you came all the way down here to tell me, I think I already know," he said.

He came off as arrogant but was the kind of guy who was sweet, deep down. He didn't rely on his looks; he was more attitude.

"It was a little bit…awesome," she said.

The thing about Scarlet was that she was usually reserved and sarcastic, but once she got to talking about music, she

became like a kid fresh off Space Mountain. She exaggerated details because that's how she experienced them—with a heightened sensibility.

"Do *you* play?" he asked.

"I do, a little, but not very well. I like to write, so that's really when I play," she said, eager to let him know they had move in common than just fashion.

"You write?"

"Yeah, you know, just lyrics and stuff."

"I have a feeling you're being modest."

"No, but I am being late," she said looking at the clock on wall. "I've gotta get to work."

"Where do you work?" he asked.

"IdentiTea, the café at old Hawthorne Manor," Scarlet said. "*The* place for chai anxiety."

"Hippie hangouts are cool," Eric said politely, but she could tell by looking at him that coffeehouses weren't exactly his thing.

"*Anyway*, the real reason I came here was to ask if you'd be into playing a gig there," Scarlet confessed. "Doesn't pay much, but I manage the place and I'm starting to promote a music night."

"Not a big deal," Eric admitted, seeming a little more interested. "I'm not in it for the money."

"Might be good exposure locally," Scarlet continued, making her case. "We have a regular crowd on Thursday nights—all ages, of course, and if you have merch you can sell after the gig."

"Cool," Eric said offhandedly, confirming the booking. "Why don't we head over to check the place out?"

"Okay, you can follow me; I'm parked right outside."

"I don't have a ride," he said. "Do you mind if I bum one from you?"

"No problem," Scarlet answered.

They walked outside to her car and continued to chat away. She could see the barest trace of a smile on Eric's face when he got a look at her car.

"Nice wheels," Eric acknowledged.

"I like it," Scarlet giggled nervously. "It's an oldie, but goodie, as they say."

As they hopped into her car, flipped on the car radio, and drove off, she took the opportunity to gather information.

"Are you staying or sleeping in the band's van or something?" Scarlet queried.

"Yeah, I'm staying around for a while," Eric said. "I've got some work to do."

"Work?" she asked. "Are you recording or something?"

"Not exactly," he said, fumbling, still really unsure of how much he could or should say to her.

"Where are you from?" Scarlet asked.

"From around here, but I left a long time ago," Eric said. "I bounced around New York and then moved to L.A. for a while."

"Make it or die trying?" she said.

"Something like that," he said.

There was a world-weary quality to Eric that Scarlet had detected from the start. He was young, but he didn't really look it or act it. Not mature, exactly, but like a guy who had done a lot of living in a very short time.

"Those are two tough towns," Scarlet said sympathetically, but really just regurgitating what she'd read in the music and fashion magazines.

"Yeah, New York is where dreams are born," Eric offered. "L.A. is where they're sold. If you're lucky."

They arrived at IdentiTea and parked, but before they got out of the car, Scarlet worked up her nerve.

"This might be a little forward of me," Scarlet said, "but I've been trying to write some songs."

"And?" Eric asked.

"I thought you might be able to help me," Scarlet said.

❧

It was a good thing, Charlotte thought, that she was good at waiting. It seemed to be taking Damen forever to return to his room, and she was getting bored. Without being too gross about it, she'd pretty much invaded every aspect of his privacy, from his closets and drawers to his notebooks and toiletry case.

Finally, she heard a key turn in the lock and the door swung open, slowly. Damen reached over to the wall for the light switch, turned it on, and closed the door behind him.

He seemed unusually tense as he dumped his backpack and a bunch of mail on his bed. He still looked great, Charlotte thought, but a bit more serious and polished than he used to. Only someone as obsessed with him as Charlotte once was would even notice, but since she'd been sent all this way back,

very much in protest at that, she felt compelled, if not obliged, to notice.

Damen's hair was trimmed a bit shorter, his jeans belted and more fitted, and his shirttail tucked in instead of hanging freely beneath his jacket and over his backside. He was always neatly dressed and appointed, but to Charlotte, he kind of looked like he was prepping for an interview. Or, heaven forbid, a date.

Suddenly, it all seemed to make sense to Charlotte. She was sent back to keep an eye on Damen, to prevent him from doing something foolish and hurtful and maybe even permanent to both himself and Scarlet. Of course! Only she knew him well enough, knew them both well enough, and cared enough to make sure that Cupid's arrow stayed on target. This was serious business, after all.

Before Charlotte even had time to appreciate the importance of her mission, Damen interrupted her thoughts with a sigh, as he picked up an envelope that had been buried.

Whatever it was, Charlotte thought, Damen was glad it had arrived. A love letter from Scarlet, maybe? She could only hope. Or someone else?

He settled down and slowly pulled the flap open, the anticipation and tension returning to his face. What was this, the Grammys? But before he could open the envelope completely, his door opened.

"Hey, man," Matt Rogers, Damen's roommate, greeted him. "I was hoping not to see you."

Matt was a blond, bespeckled frat boy. Good-looking,

smart, outgoing, athletic, and loyal, he gave a straightlaced appearance but was clearly anything but. It was obvious instantly that Damen liked him a lot.

"Sorry to disappoint," Damen shot back, "but I just might have gotten my ticket."

"No way! Open it, open it, open it…," Matt chanted, fists pumping, urging Damen on enthusiastically.

Damen took heart and bravely finished off the envelope. He reached in, grabbed the single sheet between his thumb and forefinger, and pulled it up to eye level. Even Charlotte was taken in as he read the letter silently, then looked over at his anxious roomie.

"I got it," Damen said quietly, rushing at Matt with his hand skyward for a colossal high five. "I got the internship at Hawthorne Broadcasting Studios for spring semester!"

"HBS?" Charlotte wondered. "But that's in…"

Before she could finish the thought, Matt did.

"You're going home, bro!"

They embraced in an enthusiastic man-hug for a second and then separated uneasily and shook hands firmly, with Matt getting in a last good slap to Damen's back.

"You've got an angel on your shoulder, dude," Matt said sincerely.

"I must," Damen said, already beginning to pack his stuff.

"Wonder if she's hot," Matt added.

This was the first time he ever commented about an angel being potentially hot. Usually it was either real girls in posters or comic book characters.

Damen looked at him, dumbfounded, but Charlotte was totally flattered by the compliment.

"Scarlet is going to freak," Matt said, as Damen beamed a mischievous grin back at him.

"In a good way," Charlotte thought to herself, "I hope."

Chapter 9

Sadly Beautiful

I know I'll never really get inside of you,
To make your eyes catch fire the way they should.
—The Cure

He loves me,
he loves me not.

—————◆·×·◆—————

If two past lovers remain friends, they are either still in love, or never were. We are attracted to people for all sorts of reasons; however, the human mind sometimes classifies feelings as romantic because it can't make sense of them at the given time. The truth is, those people we feel drawn to most might not be intended as love interests, but rather as life-changing, life-altering presences that come into our lives for reasons we can't yet understand.

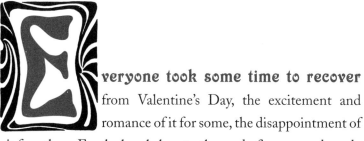**veryone took some time to recover** from Valentine's Day, the excitement and romance of it for some, the disappointment of it for others. For the lonely hearts, the cards, flowers, and candy boxes on display everywhere were like a target rash from a tick bite—an external reminder that something was very wrong on the inside. The light at the end of the tunnel, however, was prom. Just as Valentine's Day seamlessly supplanted Christmas in the stores, prom instantly uprooted Valentine's Day at school. The two were separated only by an intermittent period that unattached senior girls dubbed "hunting season" but the rest of the school knew as spring. It was official: preparation for the big day had begun. And the first step in the process for The Wendys was ditching their "kids."

"There is no way that we can get dates to the prom," Wendy Anderson sneered, "as single mothers."

"Right," Wendy Thomas said. "But we can't give them back until the end of the week. Anybody good will be taken by then," she complained.

Then, without saying a word, Wendy Anderson checked the outdoor thermometer and motioned for Wendy Thomas to follow her outside to the parking lot. They walked slowly, inconspicuously, they hoped, toward Wendy Anderson's car parked at the far end of the lot.

"Give me the kid," Wendy Anderson demanded, grabbing the doll from Wendy Thomas's grasp.

"Wendy, we'll fail!"

"Studies show that children raised by unfit teenage mothers are a burden on society," Wendy Anderson snipped. "It's our patriotic duty."

She opened the car door, proceeded to roll all the windows up and tossed both baby dolls into the backseat. Just as she was about to slam the door shut, another car pulled up right next to them.

"Hello, Dollies," Darcy said. "What's up?"

"Nothing, really," Wendy Thomas said nervously as they stood in front of the car door windows.

Darcy slid her head between them and peeked into the vehicle as The Wendys stood stiffly, cringing.

"That's a felony," Darcy exclaimed. "Why don't you send them away to 'camp' like I did?"

The Wendys instantly had visions of milk cartons and misty-eyed press conferences offering rewards and demanding that their missing "children" be found and returned.

"Thanks for the tip," Wendy Anderson said sincerely as she rescued the dolls. "Let's just keep this between us."

"No problem," Darcy said haughtily. "Speaking of secrets, how's Petula?"

"Why don't you come see for yourself?" Wendy Thomas suggested, opening a major inroad to their tight-knit circle. "We're going stalking again tonight."

"Love to join," Darcy chirped. "What should I wear?"

Before she could get another word out, The Wendys and Darcy were distracted by loud giggles and gasps coming from a gaggle of junior girls at the other end of the lot. Given the mounting prom pressure, it could only be because of a guy. They walked over to see just what the excitement was about.

"Who is *that*?" Darcy purred, nearly licking her lips.

❧

Scarlet, oblivious to the tumult making its way from the parking lot into the school, was listening to new songs she'd just demoed. She was extra happy today because the baby-return countdown widget she'd installed on her PDA showed just a few days left of parenthood. She caught sight of Petula walking toward her and tossed the doll at her.

"Think fast," Scarlet said, showing at least one thing she had in common with The Wendys: a total lack of motherly instinct.

Petula snatched it from the air and cradled it gently, shaking her head in disapproval at her sister's carelessness as they crossed paths. When she looked up and, to her surprise, saw

Damen heading her way with The Wendys just behind, she stepped around the corner to observe the situation unnoticed.

Scarlet, still lost in her music, felt an unexpected tap on her shoulder and turned around angrily, ready to lace into whoever had interrupted her playback session.

"Are you free for lunch?" Damen asked, an enormous smile breaking out across his face.

Scarlet was nearly in shock, so much so that for a second she didn't know how to respond. *What a nice surprise! Why didn't you tell me? WTF!* A million things were flooding her mind at once as a crowd of onlookers coagulated around them. But only one thing managed to escape her red-glossed lips.

"What are you doing here?" she asked, pulling out her earbuds and throwing her arms around his neck.

"I came back for the semester," Damen said. "Happy?"

Happy? Well, Scarlet thought, that was one way to put it. Astonished, confused, and a little wigged, might also do. Did he get kicked out? Did he lose his financial aid? She guessed she was about to find out and tried to slow the panic she was beginning to feel.

"Of course," she said, draping herself around him again as they walked to the cafeteria. "Why wouldn't I be?"

"That didn't sound very convincing," Darcy said to The Wendys as they strolled off in the opposite direction, with Darcy taking the lead, three steps ahead of the other two girls.

Petula, who overheard the whole thing, couldn't help agreeing. She couldn't begin to figure what was up with Scarlet's ambivalence about Damen's return, but at that second she

was distracted by a much more pressing personal matter: the departure of The Wendys and Darcy.

"A flying V?" Petula noted suspiciously as she spied them leaving. "That's *our* formation."

Charlotte hung back in the parking lot and watched Damen lead the throng into Hawthorne High as if it was a scene from some kind of old Hollywood cast-of-thousands epic. For some people, so little changes, she thought. The faces surrounding Damen were different, but the crowd itself was pretty much the same. Especially from a distance.

She remembered comforting herself when she was still alive by reading magazines about how lots of the popular high school kids peaked early, their glory days already almost behind them. Damen wasn't destined to be one of them, though. With him, it wasn't the trappings of success, football uniform, athletic ability, good looks, cool car, popular friends, or pretty girlfriend that he relied on or allowed to define him. It was just him, his essence. You didn't need to know a thing about him or where he came from to feel that.

Eric had a lot of that, as well, she thought. It was expressed differently, maybe, but the overall impression was very much the same. That's why she liked him so much, she thought as she watched Damen in action.

Charlotte laughed as she saw Pam and Prue following The Wendys and Petula, pretending to gag themselves with their stiff index fingers as they walked behind Damen.

Looking more closely, though, Charlotte realized it wasn't Petula in the lead. It was some kind of perky Petula bizarro. That made sense—Petula would never follow anyone—but it was definitely odd to see The Wendys without her. They couldn't navigate their way out of a bathtub without Petula.

Charlotte gave her curiosity a breather and decided Pam and Prue could fill her in some other time. She needed something to lift her spirit, so to speak, and the emotional hydraulic she was looking for was staring her right in the face: Dead Ed, dead ahead.

She felt a little guilty as she headed down the hallway to the basement door, but quickly assured herself that Damen would be fine without her for a while. A short climb down and then up the stairs, back into the hallway, and she was there.

The door was slightly ajar, and Charlotte peeked in, not wanting to disturb any lesson that might be in progress. But to her surprise, the room was quiet, dark, and nearly empty. She stepped in tentatively.

"Is there anybody in here?" Charlotte called out.

"Hey, you're stepping on me," a skinny, sleepy girl with big eyes and dark circles under them cried out from under Charlotte's feet.

"Oh, I'm so sorry," Charlotte winced as she looked down contritely at the groggy wraith.

"My fault," the girl said. "I was dead tired."

"Aren't we all," Charlotte jibed, feeling an instant camaraderie with the girl.

"I'm Mercury Mary," she said, perking up and offering her hand. "What brings you here?"

Mary was a total type A personality—outgoing; opinionated; and a high-protein, low-carb sort of chick. She reminded Charlotte of Pam, the way she talked and asserted herself. Charlotte liked her immediately, but thought it best not to reveal too much information to a new student.

"Honestly, I'm not sure," Charlotte said sincerely. "What about you?"

"Mercury poisoning," Mary confided. "Too many trips to the sushi bar."

"Everything in moderation," Charlotte said.

"Good advice," a voice behind her noted timidly, "but it's a little late for that now."

"It's a little late for all of us," Charlotte laughed, pulling out her favorite joke.

Unfortunately, it didn't land too well in this room. She hadn't kept in mind that these ghosts were newbies, inexperienced. They hadn't crossed over. They didn't know that it would all be okay and that it was never too late. For them, it was still a tedious and uncertain waiting game, and given the amount of empty seats in the class, Charlotte knew they might be waiting a long time.

"Are you here to save us or something?" the girl behind Charlotte asked, a tremble in her voice.

"You're safe here," Charlotte assured her, reaching for her outstretched and shaking hands and holding them tightly. "You're shaking," Charlotte said, trying her best to calm her.

"That's pretty much how she got here," Mercury Mary volunteered.

"I was startled to death by my best friend," the girl explained. "It's not that rare, statistically, at least."

"I'm Charlotte," said Charlotte in a soothing tone, "and I can promise you there's nothing to be afraid of here."

"I'm Beth," the girl responded. "But they call me Scared to Beth."

Charlotte kept her poker face, figuring she had no right to be judgmental, considering she'd been a victim of gummy-cide, which was so rare it had claimed only one victim, as far as she knew.

"I'll bet she'll never guess *my* name," the last student in class boasted, her frazzled and discombobulated expression matching her unkempt hair and wrinkly, mismatched outfit.

"That's Toxic Shock Sally," Mary advised. "She didn't know that a tampon had to be changed, um, regularly."

"It's not that I didn't know," Sally denied, embarrassed. "I just have a problem with scheduling."

"More like a problem with personal hygiene," Beth mocked.

The other girls started laughing, but Charlotte could manage only an empathetic smile. She touched Sally's shoulder in solidarity. She could see that Sally was probably not cared for very much in life. No one to brush her hair at night, to help pick out her outfits for school, to teach her about her body. The truth was, Charlotte related to her, not having had a mother to teach her these things either.

Seeing Charlotte's reaction shut the other girls up in a hurry. She considered saying something, to reprimand Beth and Mary, but every group, no matter how small, has its own dynamic, Charlotte thought. Her Dead Ed class certainly had its own "personality," with bullies, pranksters, geeks, and freaks, and once the rest of these seats were filled, this new class would too. They would find their balance on their own without her interference.

Sometimes, it occurred to her, the best way to help is to keep out of the way. So, she began to say her goodbyes.

"Don't be embarrassed," Charlotte said, looking at Sally sweetly. "I choked on a gummy bear. It doesn't get any lamer than that."

"Charlotte, what are you really doing here?" Mary asked, this time a bit more forcefully.

"Maybe she's here to teach us," Sally conjectured.

"Oh, no, I'm not qualified," Charlotte said. "I've still got a lot to learn."

❦

Damen and Scarlet were whispered about as they walked to the lunchroom, as if they were some kind of celebrity couple hitting the red carpet. Damen was not bothered, having grown accustomed to ignoring the commotion around him during his relationship with Petula. But Scarlet always hated the attention, which had only grown more fawning and intense since Homecoming.

Phone cameras were snapping the scene and textperts were

sharing the news in real time with other underclassmen who'd never seen Damen in the flesh. It was surreal, even for the teachers who also got word and stuck their heads out of their busy classrooms to see for themselves. It was like looking directly at the sun.

Damen and Scarlet took two seats in the corner of the cafeteria and sat close together. Scarlet seemed a little on edge to him, like she was spoiling for a fight. He knew the look, since he used to get it from her every time he came to pick Petula up, back in the day. Maybe Scarlet was just irritated by the admirers shuffling around the other side of the cafeteria, trying to eavesdrop on them.

As he thought of what he could do to help her relax, he noticed she was wearing an outfit she'd bought last time he was home when they went shopping together. Damen even helped pick it out. He thought that might be a good icebreaker.

"You look great," Damen cooed, reaching for her hand.

Ordinarily, a compliment from him would mean the world, but right then it just reinforced everything she wasn't liking about herself.

"Thanks," she said dismissively. "You picked it out, didn't you?"

Despite the attitude Scarlet was giving him, she loved the outfit and the fact that he'd chosen it, which was why she was wearing it. But right then, it was feeling like a prison jumpsuit.

"Nice shirt," she said of Damen's plaid cotton oxford, as

she pulled her hand from his. "On your way to Debate Club?"

"What's your problem?" he asked, taken aback.

"What's yours?" she asked derisively. "College boy."

"I *am* a college boy," Damen reminded her, hoping to defuse some of the tension. "Are you embarrassed by me or something?"

Scarlet had no idea what she was feeling or why she was being so impossible, but she really tried to stop herself.

"No," she said, ashamed of herself for doling out unwarranted criticism. "Of course not."

"You had me worried there for a minute." Damen sighed and smiled.

He still had *her* worried, she thought.

"What *are* you doing here?" she asked more sharply than she had in the hallway.

"I came to ask you to prom," Damen deadpanned.

"That's funny," Scarlet snapped, crossing her arms, tapping out seconds with her forefinger. "I'm still waiting."

Damen was only kidding about prom, but it still hurt him a little that she was so dismissive of it.

"You won," he said proudly.

"Won?" she asked, totally confused. "Did you get a job with Publishers Clearing House?"

"No," Damen chuckled, imagining himself knocking on some poor old lady's door with a camera crew and an oversize bank check. "You're a finalist in the INDY-ninety-five songwriting contest."

"Don't you have to actually enter something to win?" Scarlet asked, the anxiety rising in her throat.

"Or," Damen boasted, "you can *be* entered."

"Damen?" Scarlet asked accusingly, in a tone she might use with a small child who'd just broken a flower vase. "You didn't."

"It hasn't been announced yet," Damen went on enthusiastically, choosing to ignore the disapproving scowl that was now plastered across her face. "So just keep it quiet for now, okay?"

"Then how do you know?" Scarlet asked tersely, hoping this might be some premature April Fool's gag he was playing on her.

"I have inside information," Damen bragged. "Now that I'm an intern at the station!"

"Out of all the places to do an internship, you picked here? You could be anywhere doing something really cool."

Damen was stunned that Scarlet would diminish his achievement. They both loved the station and barely could have dreamed about working there. At the very least, Damen thought, she should have been happy that he was going to be home for the semester.

"I don't want to be *anywhere*, I want to be with you," Damen said. "I thought that was what you wanted too."

Scarlet was now at a total loss for words, but her silence was speaking to Damen loud and clear. It didn't get any better when she finally piped up.

"I am so tired of you thinking that you know what I want," she said.

He felt like he was intruding on her, as if she didn't want him around. It was now completely obvious to him, but he didn't understand why.

"Scarlet, are you seeing someone else?" Damen asked.

Chapter 10

Nobody but You

*Gravity cannot be held responsible
for people falling in love.
—Albert Einstein*

We all fall down.

———◆═✕═◆———

They call it falling for someone for a reason. Like some silent movie banana peel, love can trip you up and bring you down flat on your back when you least expect it. Either you will bounce right up, undaunted, or become paralyzed. Either way, you will carry the reminder of it forever. Whether it leaves a tiny scar or a permanent injury, only the future can tell.

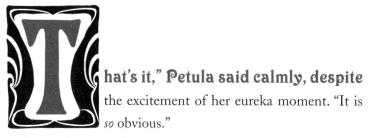

hat's it," Petula said calmly, despite the excitement of her eureka moment. "It is *so* obvious."

It wasn't exactly Stephen Hawking intuiting the theory of Everything, but it was as close to an epiphany as Petula was likely to get.

"That was hard work," CoCo exhaled, acknowledging how tough it had been to burrow into Petula's subconscious and leave a fashion mantra with her.

Petula needed some direction, some greater purpose for her late-night escapades, and CoCo was just the right soul to provide it. Suddenly, it all made sense to her.

"Look good," she recited, with CoCo mouthing along from a chair beside her bed, "feel good."

Her creative juices flowing and mind racing, Petula snuck into Scarlet's bedroom and scooped up the last bit of possible giveaways piled on her floor. Petula planned to fulfill their potential and carried them back to her room, dumping them on top of her own stack. She winced slightly at the thought of her fine threads mixing with Scarlet's but felt totally able to justify it as part of her new calling.

Then she headed for the guest room, which was next to her mom's bedroom. It was typically spare, cheaply carpeted, and underfurnished, with a few old pictures, figurines, and paintings no one wanted. It was a holding cell for stuff with just enough sentimentality to keep, but not meaningful enough to display.

Petula walked over to the closet and stood before it for a few moments before reaching for the handle. She opened the door like a coffin lid, slowly and respectfully, and took very shallow breaths through her mouth, hoping to avoid the musty odor that wafted from the enclosure. The smell of mildew passed quickly, and she began rifling through the garments hanging in front of her: a rack full of men's clothing, all but forgotten since her dad took off, leaving his wardrobe—and his family—behind.

As Petula pulled each piece forward—overcoats, cardigans, suit jackets, pants, shirts, ties, most still in the plastic from the dry cleaner's—she realized that they hadn't been forgotten at all. She could recall in greatest detail watching him walk slowly down the stairs wearing the cardigan on weekend mornings, the suit and tie as he rushed out the door to work each day, the pajamas he slipped into each night before reading her a bedtime story, the bathrobe he wore as she watched him shave with the old-fashioned brush and soap, and the powdery smell of his aftershave that filled the bathroom right afterward. As she pressed her nose to the collar, she wasn't sure if it was the actual aroma or the memory of it that still lingered after all these years. It didn't matter, she thought; she could smell it just the same.

When she was younger, she could remember arguing with her mother about keeping his things. Petula would accuse her mother of hanging on to the past, to bad memories that

would only keep her from moving on in her life. To Petula, her father's leaving was like a death — maybe even worse because it was voluntary. It was something to be gotten over and forgotten. But now, she was overjoyed and comforted that they'd kept everything. And not just kept, but preserved, like some kind of a museum exhibit of their family's past.

Petula, however, was more into living memorials and decided, with some subconscious prompting from CoCo, that it was time to resurrect them. Enough time had passed that almost everything in the closet was back in style. She gently gathered the old suits from the wooden hangers and carried them to her room.

"I know just the guy for them," CoCo thought as she watched Petula add the garments to the pile.

℞℠

The scene was set. Wendy Anderson, Wendy Thomas, and their new best friend, Darcy, were parked and ready to catch the perpetrator. The Wendys brought Darcy along primarily for third-party verification. If any of this ever leaked, no one would believe them without her corroboration. They donned their undercover '70s Bond Girl outfits, an inspired choice, and were now waiting for Petula to arrive.

"She's not the same," Wendy Anderson said, justifying the snooping.

"I think she's slowly trying to replace us, phase us out," Wendy Anderson blurted. "Well, maybe she'll be the one phased out."

"You guys are so right," Darcy spouted. "She's probably down here auditioning dropouts for a new crew."

It was something both Wendys had been thinking, but never discussed openly, until now.

"I can't wait to see who our competition is," Wendy Anderson said, but it was pretty clear from her expression that she didn't mean it.

"That's loser talk," Darcy chided as the Wendys remained on high alert, much like betrayed lovers waiting to witness the cheating firsthand. "You are The Wendys! You have no competition."

Both Wendys were so insecure about themselves and their friendship with Petula that they were always in a state of paranoia, and Petula liked it that way. She knew instinctively that both girls were strictly middle management, bereft almost entirely of leadership skills, so it was easy to keep them off-balance and constantly worrying about their place in her orbit. They supplied Petula with adulation and in return were allowed to sail along in her slipstream.

Their roles had become so entrenched, their social status—even their futures—so entangled with hers, they felt they had not just a right, but also an obligation to get to the bottom of Petula's aberrant behavior. She might be fine turning all do-goody from her coma, but they were the ones who would have to answer for it. And they found themselves unprepared. If somebody had to get knocked off the popularity pedestal, it was not going to be them.

The Wendys were bolstered by Darcy's pep talk and saw in her the motivational qualities that they were sorely missing. Darcy was ready to reign.

Pam and Prue watched this tentative mating ritual between

The Wendys and Darcy with great curiosity. Darcy had a familiar air about her, and not in a good way. Pam and Prue had developed a fondness, if not a respect, for Petula ever since the Virginia situation and didn't appreciate some new queen wannabe trying to exploit her at a vulnerable time.

"There she is!" Wendy Thomas yelled, as if she'd just discovered a rare, endangered species while on safari.

Living and dead alike watched as Petula made her way down the dark alley and toward a group of homeless kids. This amazed The Wendys, as Petula would never walk toward a group of absolute strangers without some kind of advance fanfare prepared. Pam and Prue, however, could see that she was not alone. CoCo was guiding her.

Petula plopped down the sea-green garbage bag she was toting and proceeded to size up each stranger with a tape measure. She sighed with relief when none of the haggard and undernourished girls measured bigger than a size two. Then, she reached into her bag again and again, like some kind of sartorial Santa, mixing and matching pieces of clothing into outfits for each slightly puzzled, but grateful, stranger.

"It's drive-by styling!" Wendy Anderson exclaimed, convulsing ever so slightly as she reached to the dashboard to steady herself. It was as if it was something she'd been suspecting, something she'd dreaded, even.

"Looks like it to me," Wendy Thomas said, dumbfounded.

"She's recruiting a Petula army," Darcy added, a tinge of grudging admiration in her voice.

"And we've been dishonorably discharged!" Wendy Anderson huffed.

This confirmed their worst fears. Petula was making these people into what she wanted, just like she'd done with them at first. She imprinted her brand, gave them a look and something to be proud of. They knew the feeling. They could still remember their own drive-by stylings, Petula showing up at their homes freshman year, telling them what to wear, what to eat, and when to talk.

For their basic training, Wendy Anderson remembered how Petula stripped them of their dignity, broke their spirits, and then built them back up again in her own image. It was like beauty boot camp. They did everything she said, and now look where it got them—staked out in a dark alley, watching their replacements being molded and sculpted by the master right before their false eyelashes.

The Wendys were hurt and jealous all at once. Petula was putting her personal stamp on these hard-luck cases, a blessing *they* had earned. Almost as importantly, she was giving away stuff they wanted, mostly anyway.

"She's redefining streetwear as we know it," Wendy Thomas hyperbolized, as if she were witnessing the birth of the universe.

Petula took care, as CoCo had "suggested," not just to dump the clothes off, but to really think its placement through. She was there for almost an hour, doing and redoing the looks until she got them just right. Until her subjects were totally unrecognizable. She transformed them from homeless casual to Dumpster Chic.

"Nobody will ever believe this," Wendy Anderson stammered.

"That," Darcy crowed, pulling out her digital camera, "is what night vision is for."

Darcy began snapping away with far more success than The Wendys had the night before, documenting the event like a crime scene photographer, reviewing the JPEGs in the view-finder, and deleting shots she couldn't "use," whatever that meant.

The bad vibe Pam and Prue had gotten from Darcy initially was turning seismic. She seemed to them to be absolutely giddy as she saved shot after shot.

"Check that out?" Darcy said, focusing her lens on two teary-eyed but suddenly quite fashionable young girls locked in an embrace with Petula.

"They're touching her."

The Wendys gasped in unison at the whole skeevious affair.

Petula was treating these charity cases as equals, which made them peers to The Wendys, as well. It was this involuntary downward mobility that was the last straw.

"After all you guys have done for her," Darcy said, her voice laced with pity.

"Yeah, after all we've done for her," Wendy Anderson repeated groggily, as if she was just emerging from a state of mourning.

"Yeah," Wendy Thomas agreed, shaking off her malaise as well.

"Time to make a change, girls," Darcy offered, putting her arms around both of them, as they walked back to the car. "Petula already has."

Chapter 11

The Marble Index

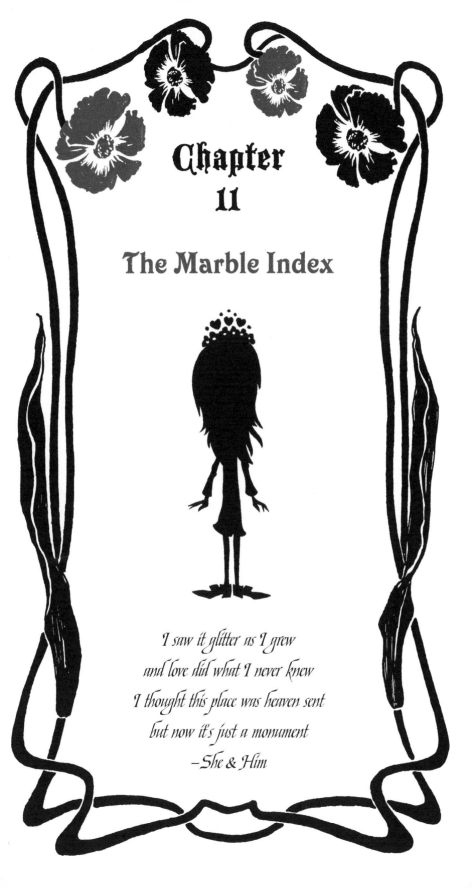

*I saw it glitter as I grew
and love did what I never knew
I thought this place was heaven sent
but now it's just a monument*
—She & Him

— · ✦ · —

There are many ways to be haunted, not all of them supernatural. From photo albums to love letters, the memory of bad choices, broken promises, lost loves, and shattered dreams can often linger far longer than the glow of satisfaction from our greatest accomplishments. Indeed, the most frightening ways to be haunted may be in the many ways we haunt ourselves.

**carlet manipulated her old key** and wiggled it just so, prompting the heavy wooden door with lead glass to open slightly. She jammed her recently unretired boot in the door, gathered her bag and the rest of her stuff, and pushed herself inside.

It was such a pain opening IdentiTea by herself on Saturdays, but she wouldn't have it any other way. She got to take advantage of the acoustics without anyone else around. During her shifts, she often did sets that became wildly popular, but she much preferred to play guitar to an empty house. In fact, before Damen went off to school, they would meet up and play together, the only two souls in the joint, but to them it felt like they were the only two in the world.

She loved how dramatic the room was with its majestic chandeliers and large carved wood features. It was such a gorgeous open space with daylight filtering in through floor-to-ceiling

lead windows, illuminating the canvas artwork, crushed velvet jewel-toned booths, wooden chairs, and intricate beamed cathedral ceiling that cast incredibly expressive shadows. The café was her place, a direct reflection of her style. It looked, she felt, the way the Dead Ed kids always saw it.

People loved it too, and came to get turned on to different music, films, and clothing. However unintentional, Scarlet was becoming a big influence in school and outside, as kids from far away carpooled to spend their Friday nights wherever she went. She was like a local celebrity, in that respect, and definitely had her followers.

Scarlet threw her bag on the counter and flicked the chandeliers on. One by one, they lit up, each with mixed jewel-toned crystals that reflected around the entire room. It made for the most amazing light show in town.

Scarlet headed up to the stage and got her guitar out—she had been neglecting it as much as she'd been neglecting everything and everyone else in her life. Then, after putting her leather-studded strap around her neck, she started thinking about Damen. She was angry with him for sharing her song with the world, or at least with the radio station, but also flattered that he thought it was good enough to enter. It was a deliriously romantic thing to do, and it showed that he really did believe in her. The thing was, Scarlet liked to do things on her own terms.

She plopped herself down on a carved wooden stool with a deep-red crushed-velvet cushion and started strumming. She hooked her iPod up to the PA system and scrolled through her playlist until she found the perfect six-string workout. She started into Agent Orange's surf punk classic "Too Young to

Die," an old favorite that she'd been listening to a lot lately. As Scarlet shredded away with gleeful abandon, she could feel the tension begin to leave her body.

She was all warmed up and wanting to run through something exciting, but she wasn't feeling any of her own stuff. The freshest music she'd heard in a while was Eric's, so she skipped to his demos, looking for some inspiration.

She was tentative at first, but soon the adrenaline was coursing through her veins again as forcefully as the current that powered her amplifier. She twisted the volume up to ten so that she could hear herself playing over Eric's song.

As she was getting really into it, when the energy was about to reach fever pitch, she noticed a guitar solo that she hadn't heard on the track before. She brushed it off, figuring she'd missed it on her first listen. Then, it happened again, only this time it sounded much more…live.

Scarlet looked around and realized that she was the only one in that dark, open space and that if someone was actually there, it would be hard to escape. All the doors were so far to the front and the windows didn't open. She jumped up, and just as she was about to run toward the door, a figure stepped out from behind the amp.

Scarlet raised her guitar over her head and readied herself to defend her life.

∾

After her pit stop at Dead Ed, Charlotte felt compelled to continue her nostalgia tour at a place where she'd never been but, ironically, would never leave either: the cemetery.

She headed directly for the unmarked section of the graveyard, it being the most likely location for her earthly remains. She needed to see it for herself, the finality of it, and she wanted to know if she had a real memorial—her name carved in limestone—or if she was just marked by a state-issued plate.

She walked through the patch, which was mostly dirt with a few islands of weeds sprouting here and there, looking downward to read the index card–size nameplates in each gray metal stake. For most of the inhabitants in the cemetery, these were temporary place keepers, marking the gravesite until a headstone could be engraved and delivered.

She walked row after row without spying a single name, just numbers, which kind of made sense, she thought. Anonymity was pretty much a prerequisite for burial in this section. She just didn't realize there were so many—what was the diplomatic phrasing here?—of the "unclaimed." The longer she perused the field the more disappointed she became, until the even more disappointing thought that she might not even be here at all crossed her mind.

Maybe they just cremated me, Charlotte thought. Charlotte had all these horrible visions of being incinerated, then scooped out of an oven and flushed down the toilet, or even worse, being "spread out on the waters" and blowing back into the hairy nostrils of some grizzled old barge skipper. She quickly did the math on the water content in the human body, determining how much of her would burn off, how much convert to ash, and what percentage of that might be permanently lodged in the snotty sinus of some sea captain, playing pattycake with all kinds of nasty rhinoviruses.

She'd just about resigned herself when she arrived at the last row of placards. Once again, she was nowhere to be found. Having come to the conclusion that she wasn't even important enough to be anonymous, she found herself at the fountain, which was shaded by the only tree in the section. A nice place to rest her soul. As she looked up slowly to eye the elaborate stone sculpture before her, she found herself face-to-face with...herself.

"It's me," Charlotte whispered, for no particular reason. "I think."

She couldn't be absolutely sure because the sculpted bust of her head was so idealized and perfect it bore little resemblance to the way she remembered herself, even considering her overhaul before senior year. It was breathtaking, she thought, even though she no longer had any breath left to give.

She read her name over and over and ran her fingers along each deeply etched letter. The ring of still fragrant and blooming roses hung around her sculpted neck added a burst of life and beauty and was proof positive that she was not just remembered, she was missed.

"Scarlet," she said, knowing full well who would have made such a gorgeous, lush gesture.

It reminded her that their relationship was something permanent, eternal. They had been so close, closer than friends, closer even than family. It was hard to know where one stopped and the other began.

Charlotte lay down on the ground, in the same position her body was buried, and stared up at the glorious sculpted monument and the sky above. It looked even bigger when viewed

from below, which was both good and bad. She felt around for her nose, trying to gauge whether it was really as big as it seemed from this angle. Apparently, it wasn't just old habits that die hard, it was body image issues, as well.

That's what's so strange about all this, Charlotte began to think as she used her thumb and index finger to measure the distance between her face and the tip of her nose. No matter how much progress she thought she'd made, it was very fragile and frighteningly easy to reverse. Perhaps that was why she was so ambivalent about being sent back to Hawthorne. She felt human there, vulnerable to all her past weaknesses and grievances and much less in control of her heart, if not her soul.

Charlotte felt the pressure of reality returning to challenge her emotionally, psychologically, and spiritually as the shadow cast by the sunset behind her monument fell over her. She did her best to fight it. If there was any place to seek peace of mind and of spirit, she thought, this was it.

It was so peaceful to lie in her very own place of rest. To close her eyes and feel her life as a distant memory. To just "be" and reflect. No worries, no obligations. She was a spirit, a part of the earth and the sky, or at least she had been before she had to return to Hawthorne. But now, the compulsion to be present, to be seen again, if only by herself, was too powerful to ignore. She looked around and saw that no one was watching, at least no one currently breathing.

Charlotte gazed up at the ring of roses and raised her invisible hand toward them, coaxing the velvety petals from the stems. They floated down, first one or two at a time and then a veritable cascade of garnet rained down on her, dusting her face and

hair and legs like confectioner's sugar on a gingerbread man. She raised each limb into the floral typhoon and watched the petals cling to them; whether by the force of her own ghostly will or electromagnetism made no difference to her.

"I'm still here," Charlotte whispered to herself, satisfied.

As the last rose petals dropped through the moist air, Charlotte noticed a weathered plastic bag that had been tucked behind the flowers but hidden from her view until now. She sat up and reached for it, quickly opening the baggie, and was shocked to see her name scribbled on the envelope inside, in the same troubled handwriting she'd seen on Damen's wall. Charlotte could feel the sheet of folded paper inside the envelope.

She removed it and started unfolding the letter slowly and a bit tentatively. As the piece of paper grew larger and larger in width and length in her grasp, Charlotte expected to see a torrent of words and emotions spill from the damp page. But each upturn of the tightly creased flaps only revealed more blank space, leaving Charlotte even more anxious and confused. That is until the sheet was completely opened and three small, faintly written words in the very bottom corner of the page were detected.

Who am I? was all it said.

It was left *with* her, Charlotte thought, but it was not *for* her.

This kind of soul-wrenching uncertainty was really familiar territory for Charlotte, but not for Scarlet. Scarlet's confusion about herself, her past, her future, even about Damen. It was all in those three words. Charlotte's intuition

about the photos in Damen's dorm room had been right on, she thought.

Without Charlotte, Scarlet literally had no one to share herself with. Maybe that's why Scarlet was reaching out to the point of leaving a letter dangling from her headstone. Charlotte knew Scarlet would say a therapy session was just like talking to a brick wall anyway, so she might as well confide in a piece of stone with her best friend's face on it. It was flattering but disconcerting, just the same.

Charlotte came looking for her place of rest and found anything but. The reasons for her return were becoming clearer, but there was only one problem: if Scarlet was in such distress, why wasn't she assigned to help her?

She kissed her granite self goodbye gently on the cheek and walked out of the cemetery to find Scarlet.

❧

Charlotte approached Hawthorne Manor, which was as stately and gleaming as ever in her eyes. Before entering the ground-floor café, Charlotte felt a wave of anxiety surge through her. She had forced herself to bury how much she missed Scarlet, as a kind of self-defense mechanism. But now, having shed the peaceful ambience of the Other Side, however temporarily, she was free to feel the anticipation of seeing her kindred spirit, her soul mate. Charlotte needed Scarlet more than ever, and if Scarlet couldn't see her, sense her, or feel her, it would be devastating.

Charlotte walked up to the door and paused. She was curious about so many things, including what Scarlet would be

wearing. How superficial was that, she admonished herself? Charlotte peeked excitedly through the glass-paned door, and her jaw dropped. Scarlet was in full attack mode, wielding her guitar overhead, ready to strike at Eric. There wasn't much potential for harm since Eric was already dead. So, the main issue Charlotte was having was seeing them together, her best friend and her boyfriend. And the fact that Scarlet could see Eric only made things worse.

"Careful with that ax, Scarlet," Eric chuckled, raising his hands in front of his face and pretending to be afraid. "You could kill someone."

"You're the one who ought to be careful," Scarlet chided. "I'm pretty good with this thing."

"You sure are," he said, acknowledging both her guitar playing and her swordsmanship. "I thought you told me you played a *little*."

They both smiled. Scarlet was impressed that Eric had kept his cool and brushed the whole thing off, even managing to compliment her guitar playing in the process. But she still had questions, like what was he doing there in the first place.

"How did you get in?" she asked. "It's hard enough for me to get that huge door open with a key."

"I have my ways," he said vaguely.

She was sure that he did.

Her mind started to flood with jailhouse scenarios about how some veteran criminal might have schooled him in the art of breaking and entering. After all, she really didn't know Eric. He could be some deranged stalker, not just a killer guitar player but a plain old killer. Horrible news reports started

broadcasting live from her brain and everything started to go in super-slow motion, except for her racing heart.

"You're not afraid of me, are you?" Eric asked.

She raised her eyebrows, showing neither worry nor confidence.

"Relax," he said, sensing her tension. "I came in through the bathroom window. You said you'd be here, and I didn't want to wait in the rain."

"I said I'd be here when the place was open," Scarlet said, making a mental note to check the shutters from now on.

"I wanted to try out the PA system with no one here," he explained. "That's the only way to really gauge the true sound of a room."

She could totally relate to that, seeing that she lived for playing in that empty space. It was almost as if he could read her thoughts. Anyway, he seemed to have a good answer for everything; so either he was clairvoyant, a genius homicidal maniac with an acoustics fetish, or…he was telling the truth.

"Well, no point in wasting a good opportunity," Scarlet said, slinging her guitar back around her shoulder. "Can you teach the song to me?"

"I guess," Eric agreed, strumming the intro chords to his song with Scarlet watching his hands closely and following along.

They thrashed away, trading solos and screaming lyrics, lost in the music and the moment.

Charlotte couldn't believe it was Scarlet up there jamming with her boyfriend. She was cool as ever in leggings and a vin-

tage tee dress. Her super-straight do bounced along to every head-banging power chord. Eric head-banging alongside her in his black denim drainpipes and red high-top Chucks. In Charlotte's eyes, they looked like the perfect couple—a seasoned punk duo making a beautiful noise.

She genuinely didn't want to be angry, but it was hard to keep her insecurities from running wild any longer. She was nearly crushed by the sight of them, laughing and having fun. They were so original and unique, but they seemed to belong together like two drumsticks on a snare.

The last few notes sounded from their amplifiers, and Scarlet looked up at the clock to see that opening time was fast approaching. The expression on their faces confirmed that they'd both had a blast, so much so that there wasn't even a need to say it.

"Let's do this again sometime," Eric said, half-joking.

"Great," Scarlet responded, on a total melodic high. "What about coming back to play during business hours?"

"With you?" Eric asked, putting her on the spot.

"Maybe," she answered coyly.

Their banter made Charlotte feel sick inside, like she'd just been told she had some fatal, incurable, drug-resistant virus that would eat the flesh off her bones. If she had any color, it would have drained from her face entirely. Then Eric uttered the words that pushed Charlotte over the emotional edge.

"Cool," he said. "It's a date."

Chapter 12

Burning from the Inside

Who's going to make me forget you
And get you off my mind?
I could be out breaking other people's hearts
If you weren't still breaking mine.
— Kirsty MacColl

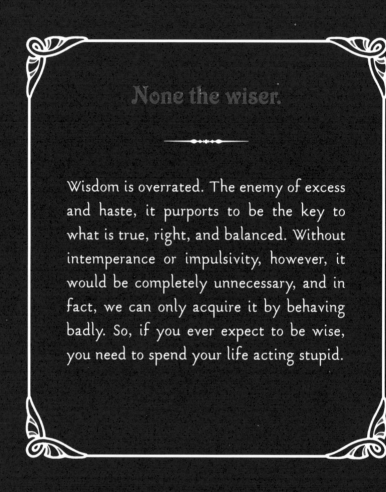

None the wiser.

Wisdom is overrated. The enemy of excess and haste, it purports to be the key to what is true, right, and balanced. Without intemperance or impulsivity, however, it would be completely unnecessary, and in fact, we can only acquire it by behaving badly. So, if you ever expect to be wise, you need to spend your life acting stupid.

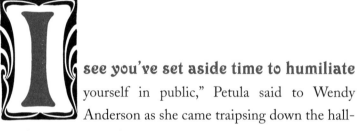"**see you've set aside time to humiliate** yourself in public," Petula said to Wendy Anderson as she came traipsing down the hallway in a vintage punk tee.

At closer inspection, Petula realized that it was a tee that Scarlet had thrown out and that she had given to someone on the street. Her heart sank. The Wendys were about to become wet-gloss whistle-blowers.

"Like my new or, I mean, my old shirt?" Wendy Anderson said, looking Petula straight in the eye, something she rarely did.

"The jig is up," Wendy Thomas said. "Soon everyone will know that you've been slumming it."

"I've been slumming it for years with the both of you and no one seemed to mind that," Petula snapped.

The Wendys tried to roll with the blow but couldn't escape the range of Petula's verbal shrapnel.

"If you start spreading lies about me, I'll just have to start telling the truth about both of you."

Petula knew that The Wendys were easily distracted, particularly susceptible to reverse psychology, and that the more she challenged them, the faster they'd back down — and probably turn on each other.

"What truth?" Wendy Thomas asked.

"Exactly," Petula said, knowing that she didn't have anything on the girls, but figuring that The Wendys would find something to accuse each other of later.

The Wendys began eyeing each other suspiciously, as expected.

"You know, I really wish I had a lower IQ so that I could enjoy your company more," Petula said to both of them, cocking her head back for effect.

The Wendys took this personally since Petula had always questioned the accuracy of this kind of scoring. In fact, she believed that the only real measure of smarts was real-life results. Thus, she'd trained The Wendys in the art of using their anatomical gifts to attract attention as a means of achieving the highest possible grades. Petula called these assets their "learning curves."

"Breaking news," Wendy Thomas announced. "Standardized testing is a flawed measure of intellectual ability."

For a change, Petula realized that Wendy's factoid carried some weight. She'd done her job well. Too well.

"Even so," Wendy Anderson added, "we're still smart enough to know a future bag lady when we see one."

She pulled the abandoned T-shirt down, stretching it out for Petula to see it clearly.

"Is that all you've got?" Petula pressed. "Huh?"

"It's not all *I've* got," a voice sounded from behind.

Petula spun around to see Darcy, smirking and fingering the advance button on her digital camera. Petula just glared as Darcy walked around to join The Wendys, and completed the wedge.

"What is this?" Petula eyed the trio, hands on jutted hips. "Stunt casting?"

If it was, even Petula had to admit they'd done a good job. Darcy had many of Petula's qualities and all the characteristics that she loved in her stooges, except for one: she was not a follower. Petula was fascinated at the move being made against her.

"You don't replace us," Wendy Anderson scoffed, gesturing toward Darcy like a new refrigerator on a daytime game show. "We replace you!"

"What I did or didn't do," Petula answered carefully, "is my affair."

"I didn't say you were cheating," Wendy Thomas huffed.

"You aren't even dating." Wendy Anderson sought to dis. "Everyone knows that."

Petula could only stare in amazement.

"It's not just your business," Darcy intervened, coming to their defense. "They have to answer for it too."

Judging from the crowd of kids gathered around them, most of whom were eyeing Petula with a mix of confusion and condescension she'd never experienced before, Darcy wasn't far off. Petula remained indignant nevertheless, choosing to invoke the tried-and-true "So what?" defense.

"So sue me, bitches," Petula scoffed, flipping them off as she departed.

"Now there's an idea," Darcy said to her disheartened new followers.

๛

Damen wanted to see Scarlet, but it was very late, so he decided to play the romantic, and sneak in and surprise her. He approached the house, with Charlotte, still seething from the little Scarlet-and-Eric jam session she'd spied on earlier, unknowingly in tow. Through the window, he could see her listening to music on her bed and flipping through a book, as usual. The tunes from her stereo speakers were blaring so loudly, she didn't notice anything else, not even Damen and Charlotte peering in at her through the window.

Damen stood there for a minute admiring her, and Charlotte could see that it was the look of real, genuine love. She had longed to be gazed at like that, to be adored, and she thought she might be on her way to that undiscovered country with Eric. It was more than a little ironic to her that Scarlet, of all people, might be the roadblock in the way of that journey.

Damen tapped on the window, but Scarlet couldn't hear him with the music blasting. He didn't want to knock any louder and alert her mother or Petula, so he waited, a bit foolishly, for the song to be through. He started tapping at the fade-out and finally managed to get her attention. It was a weird, almost sad scene, Charlotte thought. She was feeling too uncomfortable to stay but too curious to leave.

"Who's there?" Scarlet asked, slamming her book shut as she jumped off the bed.

Damen just smiled, completely oblivious to the fact that he was the second guy of the day to surprise Scarlet, and waited for his warm welcome.

"You scared the crap out of me," she said. "Why didn't you text me to tell me you were coming?"

"I wanted to surprise you," he said.

"With a heart attack?"

Hadn't he learned that his surprises weren't really working out? Scarlet thought.

"I just wanted to see you," Damen said.

"Get in here before my mother finds you and rips out a never-seen-before internal organ."

Damen climbed through the window and looked at her.

"Is it Halloween, already?" he joked.

"What?"

"Your tee," he said, referring to the band tee she was wearing.

"That's funny, you used to like it," she snipped.

Charlotte knew where all this was going, at least she thought so, and more importantly she knew why.

Scarlet was wearing one of her old band tees, the Plasmatics, but she cut the top and sleeves off, reinventing it as a halter, with one asymmetrical strap holding it up across her chest to her back. Her old self was fighting its way back. And winning.

"What's gotten into you?" Damen asked, taken aback by her criticism.

"You have," she said.

"You're taking this the wrong way," Damen explained, a bit haplessly. "I only said that because you haven't worn those tees in a while, so I thought you were getting them back out again for a reason."

"Yeah, there's a reason, actually," she said, biting her lip from unloading on him completely.

It was almost as if Scarlet was forcing a reaction from him so she could speak her mind. As if she was looking to replay an argument that she'd already had—and won—in her mind. Charlotte wished that there was something she could do. She felt so…helpless.

"Sorry, I didn't know this stalker post was taken," a voice called from the darkness.

It was Eric. He came around the back of the tree and revealed himself to Charlotte.

"I was wondering where you were," Charlotte said, both asking and scolding him at the same time.

"So, this is how you spend your nights?"

"It's actually not; I spend them with him," she said, referring to Damen. "It's obviously how you spend yours, though."

"Why are we doing this?" Eric asked. "Are you actually jealous of a living girl?"

"No," Charlotte said unconvincingly.

His acknowledgment actually made things worse, and the fact that he brought up Scarlet was proof, she surmised, that he had something to hide. She knew nothing could ever come of it, but his having feelings toward Scarlet hurt just the same, if not worse.

"Come on, this is crazy," Eric said dismissively. "I didn't die for her like you did for him. Don't forget that."

"You make it sound so...," Charlotte began.

"True?" he said, finishing her thought.

Chapter 13

The Obsolete Girl

Lose yourself, lose your audience.
—Noel Coward

Superiority complex.

Bad news is good news. Few things satisfy us as fully as the comedown of someone we dislike, or someone we do like, or even someone we don't even know. We eat it up like a scandalous tabloid story, a "without makeup" photo, or even mildly juicy local gossip. Nothing sells like failure.

etula approached her locker cautiously, more than a little suspicious of the pink envelope jutting from it. It could be a letter bomb, she thought, considering the way things had been going. She reached for it slowly, grasped it quickly, and ran her manicured index finger under the flap, opening it. It didn't detonate, but Petula was ready to explode as she pulled out the pink and purple card inside. It was an invitation, handwritten in girlish sixth-grade-print style.

YOU ARE OFFICIALLY SUBPOENAED TO A
TRIAL PARTY FOR PETULA KENSINGTON
TODAY
4:00 P.M.
HAWTHORNE HIGH GYMNASIUM
RSVP TO WENDY ANDERSON OR WENDY THOMAS VIA TEXT

Petula was livid. Who were these three wanna-me's to convene a popularity inquest? By what authority, Petula wondered, since she was the only one with the power to order such an inquiry. She grabbed her things and stomped off to the gym, ready for battle.

❧

Hawthorne High was eerily quiet after last period. The buses were empty and the parking lot was filled with parked cars. No stereos blasting, no curse words being tossed about, no nothing. All the activity was centered on the gymnasium, where weeks from now, the prom would go down and memories would be made; but today, history of a very different sort was on the slate.

A Who's Who of Hawthorne glitterati, all of whom seemed to have a vested interest in the success or failure of the current social leadership, filed into the gym. The students packed the bleachers from top to bottom, leaving the very bottom row, which was taped off, open, for what, remained to be seen. They sat there quietly, all anticipating…something.

Slowly but surely, things began to happen. The Wendys and Darcy arrived, pushing dramatically through the gym doors like TV court show litigants, dressed in nearly identical navy two-piece pinstriped power suits with the recently recovered vintage band tees underneath, hard-shell briefcases, spike heels, black retro Lady Clubman eyeglass frames with nonprescription lenses, and their hair twisted up in tight buns.

They took their seats at one empty table, leaving little doubt about whom the sole chair at the empty table across from them was reserved for.

Pam and Prue followed them, instantly taken with the ominous tone of the room.

"I feel like we are about to witness a hit-and-run," Prue said.

"You would know," Pam jibed.

They settled in and waited, along with the crowd.

After rifling through, though not really examining, her papers, Wendy Anderson walked over and searched the bleachers for volunteers for the jury. From the awesome response to their invites, The Wendys were confident that they could stack the entire panel in their favor with ambitious Junior Varsity cheerleaders, all of whom could benefit directly from The Wendys' goodwill and patronage. Sure enough, there was no shortage of volunteers happy to ensure a rush to judgment. With the jury selected and seated, anticipation for the main event built to a fever pitch. And Petula did not disappoint.

As the doors opened slowly, the entire crowd fell silent. Petula took a few steps in and stopped to assess the surreal scene facing her from the other side of the gym. She'd never been so alone, and for many in the audience, had never been seen alone either. Where The Wendys would have been dutifully trailing behind her, she had only her shadow in tow. Even CoCo, still assembling outfits for the next run downtown, hadn't arrived to provide invisible support. Literally, no one had her back.

Petula approached the empty seat facing the audience and directly opposite Darcy and The Wendys. She refused to give her accusers the satisfaction of looking directly at them and instead stared over them at the peanut gallery waiting

patiently in the bleachers. It was the kind of gathering Petula might have assembled in her own honor, filled with the cream of the crop, by Hawthorne's small-town standards, all perfectly willing to step on or over each other on their way up the populadder. At least The Wendys had learned something from her, she thought.

She walked toward the tables and felt something she'd never felt before. A wave of self-consciousness crashed over her. She could feel the eyes of her classmates on her, picking her apart. A less proud person might have acknowledged the panic beginning to set in, but Petula had no experience with anxiety and instead put her jitters down to a chitosan colon cleanser she'd had before last period.

As Petula took her seat, Darcy stood up and called the proceedings to order, removing one shoe and slamming the spike heel down in front her, like a gavel.

"The case of the Hawthorne High Populazzi vs. Petula Kensington is now in session," Darcy announced.

Although this was really an impeachment trial, The Wendys preferred to make it a class action suit, assuming there was strength in numbers and that their motives might seem less personal and petty. Petula rolled her eyes in disgust and stared daggers at them for the first time since entering the gymnasium. To her surprise, she was unable to intimidate them. They were all business.

"You have the right to remain silent," Wendy Anderson advised, confusing an arrest with a trial.

"I know my rights," Petula responded. "Let's get on with it."

"You are hereby charged with actively seeking to ruin The

Wendys' hard-earned reputation by consorting with all manner of lowlifes, dropouts, and losers," Darcy began. "And of depriving The Wendys of their rightful inheritance as your heirs in the Hawthorne High social scene by replacing them with aforementioned skeeves."

Petula forced herself to listen carefully to the charges. As far as she could tell, they had no idea what she was really up to downtown, which was fair enough, since she barely did either. Her best move, she surmised pragmatically, was to say little, but to say it defiantly.

Pam and Prue were also listening intently, hoping for some clue to help them better understand what they were supposed to be doing. The more they heard, the more they found their focus shifting to Darcy. The Wendys were shallow and petty, to be sure, but Darcy was malicious. She was enjoying turning the screws on Petula, a girl she barely even knew.

"How do you plead?" Darcy asked.

"Not guilty," Petula replied arrogantly.

"Objection!" Wendy Anderson interjected, stomping her foot like a spoiled child.

"You are too!" Wendy Thomas shot back, apparently not fully grasping the concept behind the presumption of innocence.

"Prove it," Petula challenged smugly. "And you'd better have more on me than my sister's T-shirts."

Darcy took the cue. She pulled up digital pictures and video clips on her digicam and cell phone and texted them one by one to her buddy list, which just so happened to be everyone in attendance. Petula thought about challenging

the admissibility of the surveillance images on constitutional grounds, since taking the pictures was potentially an invasion of her privacy rights, but quickly decided that this situation probably didn't rise to that level.

"These," Darcy informed the jury, "were taken downtown the other night."

As photo after photo loaded into cell phones, jaws dropped and gasps of surprise filled the room. There was proof positive of Petula lavishing attention and designer threads on a gaggle of grateful street dwellers. Oddly, the only person in the room smiling was Petula, whose placid expression, even more than the photographic evidence, revealed the pride and satisfaction she had taken in her handiwork. She couldn't help herself.

"Every picture tells a story," Darcy smirked, confident she'd given the jury sufficient reason to believe.

"And every dog has its day," Petula warned weakly. "Or should I say every bitch?"

"Objection," Wendy Thomas popped off. "That's hearsay."

The irony that The Wendys, who could give a tutorial in gossip, were using "hearsay" as a defense of Darcy was not lost on Petula. It was now plainly obvious to her that this trial was for show. Nothing she was going to say would affect the predetermined outcome. The verdict was inevitable.

Nevertheless, a certain sense of relief at being outed began to fill her as she remained silent.

"The prosecution rests," Darcy exclaimed.

"Your turn," Wendy Anderson said grudgingly, pointing at Petula.

Petula did not respond and looked up again at the crowd,

almost sympathetically. She could see their minds had been made up as well. It's not that they were particularly hard-hearted or uncharitable kids, it's just that people like them occupied a certain role inside and outside of school.

Their obligation to the needy was to host self-financing fund-raisers and put together bake sales, dance marathons, kissing contests, and the like that usually resulted in phantom proceeds. The main purpose of the events was to "raise aware-ness," not to actually relieve suffering but to make everyone aware that you cared about the problem—from a distance.

Petula's big sin was that she'd gotten her hands dirty, figu-ratively and literally. The kind of aid she was providing was specific and personal. Anybody could throw together a coat drive, she thought. This dealt with the surface issue of pro-tecting against the elements—important work—but also put some ego and color back into their lives.

Petula was a big believer not just in her own superiority, but in her innate exceptionalism. She had an unconditional self-love that she found profoundly lacking in most everyone around her. It had given her tremendous power over others, The Wendys to be specific. Now, she thought, trying to share it, confer it on those most in need of it, would be her undoing. She was beginning to have second thoughts about all of it as she waited for the ax, or rather the heel, to fall.

With Petula twisting in the wind, Scarlet happened to breeze by the gym on her way to the parking lot. She peeked in the door, figuring the Prep committee was always good for a few laughs, but what she saw was definitely not funny. At first, it looked like Petula might be conducting some kind of

how-to-dress-for-your-body-type prom seminar, but the vibe
was a little too grim for that. Scarlet looked a little closer and
spied The Wendys wearing her T-shirts and Darcy standing in
full prosecutorial mode. Scarlet had not seen her sister appear
so vulnerable since she was in a coma.

"What the hell?" was all she could eke out as she hid behind
the door and listened.

After a few moments of silence, it was obvious Petula would
not speak on her own behalf.

"Nothing to say for yourself?" Darcy asked Petula.

Darcy turned to the crowd, inviting their participation and
seizing the moment to instigate a full-on public repudiation
of Petula.

"How about you guys?" she added, cajoling the mob behind
her. "Anything to add?"

The sense of betrayal was evident in their mocking voices
as all kinds of nastiness rained down on Petula from the cheap
seats. Homecoming this was not.

"We made you, and we can break you!" a shout came from
the crowd.

"You are a just a bunch of bleach and labels," a girl vented.

"Thank you," CoCo said, scoping out the heckler, as she
strolled into the chaotic scene.

Pam whistled to get her attention and waved for her to
come over.

"What have I missed?" CoCo asked, curious as ever about
the misfortunes of others.

By the looks on Prue's and Pam's faces, CoCo got her
answer.

The three spirits returned their attention to the terrible tribunal.

"Everyone who doesn't like Petula anymore, raise their hands," Wendy Anderson ordered, raising her own left arm, palm up, fingers spread widely.

Virtually everyone followed suit as an instant forest of limbs sprang up. There was no need to count. The bleachers looked like a group ad for underarm deodorant.

"Majority rules," Wendy Thomas noted snidely, stating the obvious. "Case closed."

"You have been found guilty of abdicating your role as our leader," Darcy proclaimed.

Petula kept mum. Darcy sat down and turned to one Wendy, then the other, whispering and pointing at Petula as they scrolled through the cell phone pictures. They then turned to the J.V. jury for their decision. After a short deliberation, a note was passed to the popularity prosecutors and the inevitable was announced.

"Petula Kensington, please rise," Darcy requested.

Petula stood, facing her nemesis, crossed her arms in front of her, and sucked in her cheeks, as the crowd weighed in for good measure.

The Wendys, who had been busily scribbling away on their index cards, jumped up and read Petula's sentence.

"The name of Petula Kensington will be removed from all prom posters and programs, invitations and floats, and from every school newspaper and yearbook ad," Wendy pronounced. "In addition, she will be stripped of all authority over the cheerleading and pom-pom squads, disinvited from

all parties and pep rallies, and prohibited from speed dialing, instant messaging, texting, socially networking, or communicating with us, by any means."

"I'm de-listed?" Petula asked skeptically, suddenly feeling like a worthless stock on the popularity exchange.

"D-Listed," Darcy sniped.

Call it what she liked, the facts were that she was now rendered obsolete. Overthrown by the very kiss-asses she'd once ruled.

"This trial is adjourned," Darcy announced, once again striking the tabletop with her high-heeled shoe.

Petula remained standing, stock-still, as The Wendys and Darcy grabbed their things and left in formation, followed by the crowd, who filed past, refusing to look at her. The only acknowledgment of her existence, a few disapproving mumbles.

For the first time in her life, Petula Kensington was invisible.

❧

Charlotte sat waiting for Scarlet to arrive home from school. She'd held off as long as she could. Whether it was out of fear that Scarlet might not be able to see her anymore, or had outgrown their friendship, or that she was intimidated by Scarlet's growing chemistry with Eric was no longer important. She needed to talk to her. Privately. No Damen. No Eric.

She let her feet dangle from Scarlet's bed for a while, and looked the room over, the contents of Scarlet's letter playing over and over in her head. It felt very different. There was no

new furniture, but most of what was there had been reupholstered and repositioned.

The space seemed bigger and brighter, more open and less cluttered than she remembered. The word Charlotte was looking for, which Scarlet would really hate, was sleeker. The changes were subtle but significant and seemed to Charlotte to be in keeping with the image in the photo she'd seen in Damen's dorm room.

The best measure of where Scarlet was emotionally, however, always was her wardrobe. Charlotte made a beeline for Scarlet's closet and rummaged through the gorgeous frocks she had accumulated. Long gone were most of the tees and hoodies she was known for, with just a few managing to make the cut.

This, it occurred to Charlotte, was one of the few things about being a ghost that was so cool. Who wouldn't want to poke their head, unseen, into someone's life? It was like eavesdropping, on steroids. There was so much to learn about someone. Without all the emotional filters and facades, you could experience who a person really was, not who they wanted you to think they were. In the case of a friend, however, there are some things it is better not to know. People change, Charlotte thought. What if Scarlet *had* outgrown her, just like her band tees? Out of sight, out of mind.

Charlotte continued to torment herself for what seemed to be an eternity, when she heard the doorknob, an antique rose crystal job she'd always admired, jiggle. Charlotte wanted to speak, to screech, anything, but she couldn't make a sound.

Scarlet walked into the room, threw her car keys and bag onto her bed, and walked right past Charlotte, who was

propped up, eagerly waiting to be acknowledged. Charlotte was devastated, deflated. How could she make it though all this stuff with Eric, be back on earth—back at Hawthorne, no less—and not have Scarlet to confide in? Her worst fear had officially come true.

Charlotte plopped herself back on Scarlet's bed. She just wanted to snuggle up and bury herself with pillows; she wanted to hide.

"Hey, don't get your dead juice on my new coverlet," Scarlet said while fixing her hair in her art deco vanity.

Charlotte was confused.

"You heard me," Scarlet said, looking behind her through the mirror.

Scarlet turned around and pounced on the bed next to Charlotte, almost tackling her.

"I thought…," Charlotte began, trying to wrestle back, but still stunned.

"I know what you thought," Scarlet said. "It took everything out of me just to walk past you!"

Charlotte needed Scarlet for lots of things, but this reminded her that she needed her for something else—some comic relief.

Scarlet smiled a crooked smile and then fell into a heap on her bed.

"What are you doing here?" Scarlet nearly screamed.

"I got your note," Charlotte said, smiling sweetly at her friend.

There was so much more Charlotte wanted to tell her, but she decided it was best not to just then.

Scarlet, for her part, was relieved and embarrassed. She never expected Charlotte to get the note, but she was glad she did and gladder still to see her best friend. If anyone understood the ups and downs of the whole "change" thing, and more importantly, understood Scarlet, it was Charlotte.

Without any further prompting, she started spilling her guts to Charlotte.

"You're the only one I can talk to," she said, getting uncharacteristically emotional. "And you're gone."

"I'm here now," Charlotte comforted, sweeping Scarlet's bangs from her lashes. "Talk to me."

Scarlet hesitated. Letting everything out would make it much more real. But if ever there was a person to trust, it was Charlotte. Scarlet kept it simple, knowing Charlotte would understand.

"I'm losing myself," she said, wiping the tears from her hazel eyes.

The pain of the admission was almost as hard for Charlotte to hear as it was for Scarlet to speak, but she'd gathered as much from Scarlet's letter. If there was one thing that was never in doubt when it came to Scarlet, it was her sense of self.

"Look at me," she went on, offering herself for inspection.

Charlotte could tell how fragile Scarlet was, so she proceeded with caution. No need to mention the pictures in Damen's room that had tipped her off to all of this.

"Well, it just looks like you've grown up a bit, but I can see the old you," she explained.

"Can you?" Scarlet sniffed. "Where?"

"In here," Charlotte said, pointing to her heart. "You're always the same."

They embraced, reminded of the bond they shared. Scarlet was touched but still not ready to let it go.

"Be honest," Scarlet said. "Do I look like the old me to you?"

Scarlet was pressing Charlotte, hoping for some objectivity. After all, they hadn't seen each other for a while, so she would be the perfect person to make a before-and-after evaluation.

"What is all this obsessing with the 'old me'?" Charlotte asked. "That's what's really new."

"It's just because I've been reminded of a lot of things I used to love, used to be, by someone," she said.

"Someone?" Charlotte asked, knowing full well who that someone was.

Scarlet brushed off the question, obviously not willing to share that relationship with Charlotte.

"I just feel like I've made all these changes," Scarlet explained. "And I don't know who I am anymore."

"Did you do all this for Damen?"

"It's not that he ever asked," Scarlet explained, her voice trailing off along with her thought.

"Then maybe this is just about you," Charlotte offered, "growing up."

As soon as the words left her lips, Charlotte knew this was not the best thing to say. Scarlet lashed out.

"What would you know about that?" Scarlet snapped, immediately wishing she could take it back as well.

Both girls eyed each other apologetically.

"I'm just not happy, Charlotte," she said. "Damen's this preppy college guy and I've been trying to keep up but I don't know if we *fit* anymore."

Scarlet paused for a moment, letting what she'd just blurted out sink in.

"He's not a shirt," Charlotte said.

"We're just in different places, and I don't know if I can bridge that gap."

"Or maybe you don't know if you want to," Charlotte suggested, barely disguising the worry in her voice.

"Maybe," Scarlet said flatly.

Chapter 14

Sweet the Sting

You talk to me as if from a distance
And I reply with impressions chosen
From another time
—Brian Eno

Assumptions are the death of a relationship.

If you think you know what's going on inside someone else's head, think again. We imagine that love gives us the power to read one another's mind, when all we are really doing is reading our own. It's a great self-defense mechanism but no substitute for actual communication. The best way to know what's really on someone's mind is also the riskiest: you have to ask them.

**harlotte found herself alone with** Damen again, his sole companion as he worked the phone lines on the radio station's graveyard shift. *Worked* was probably not the right word, as the board had yet to light up once. *Watched* the phone lines was more like it. Charlotte knew this feeling all too well from her first days at the intern hotline, but she also knew that if you waited, something would eventually happen.

It was no secret that there was a time she'd have killed a small animal to be this close to Damen in a private, sound-proof room during his radio overnight. But now, so much had changed. Though she could never completely forget the flutters and twinges of her first love, the days of her schoolgirl devotion were long gone. The bittersweet yearning that she'd felt for Damen in life was now replaced by plain old sadness. Not because she wanted him, but because Scarlet apparently didn't.

There he was, sitting behind the console, trying desperately to put together a few thoughts on paper that might reach her in a way his words could not. He wanted her to know how he felt about her, that he never wanted to change anything about her. That he loved her for who she was and everything she was going to be.

Charlotte sat there helplessly, witnessing the heart-wrenching struggle. Damen was vulnerable and in pain, and it hurt her to see him going through this. She began feeling very much like the friend who plays both sides, except she wasn't playing either yet.

He was her assignment, so she must have been brought here to help him in some way. Salvaging his relationship with Scarlet was a pretty good guess, she thought. Back when she was in Dead Ed, she had guided his hand to check off the right boxes and pass a physics test, but coaxing the emotions out of his heart and onto the page seemed far beyond even her own ghostly powers.

But in order to help him, she needed to put some skin in the game, so to speak. She needed to make her presence known in some clever way that wouldn't completely freak him out.

Suddenly, the blinking light on the console interrupted her strategy session and Damen leapt into action like a bench-warmer substituting for an injured player. He had a live one, literally.

"INDY-Ninety-five, we're the difference, what's your problem?" he said in the raspiest, quiet-storm voice he could muster.

The line was engaged but quiet.

"Hello?" he asked, a bit louder.

This time he could hear the sound of whimpering coming through.

"What's your name?" Damen asked gently.

"Anais," she said, still teary. "What's yours?"

"Damen," he said, reverting to his radio voice. "Your helpful host tonight on 'What's Your Problem?'"

"My problem is my boyfriend," the caller said frankly.

"Okay," Damen said nervously.

He was totally unprepared for this kind of call. He had barely gotten through Psych 101 his first semester and couldn't even write a letter to his own girlfriend, let alone comfort someone else's. Charlotte, on the other hand, sensed an opportunity and placed a call of her own.

"Polly?" Charlotte asked, telepathically calling back to the intern office. "You've got to connect me to someone."

"I knew you wouldn't be able to hold out," Polly said. "Booty calls are technically toll-free, but they will take their toll, so be selective, girlfriend."

"No, not that kind of call," Charlotte said to Polly's disappointment. "Listen, is anybody on the line with a girl named Anais?"

"Yep, I am," Polly said, curiously. "Why?"

"Oh, she's just someone I know," Charlotte said. "Would you mind transferring the call to me?"

"Okay," Polly said. "But she's a total basket case, calling into late-night love lines, the whole deal."

Charlotte wasn't interested in putting words in Anais's mouth as much as getting into Damen's head.

"So, you'll connect me?"

"Gladly," Polly agreed with a giggle. "Don't do anything I wouldn't do."

That was a piece of advice Charlotte definitely planned to ignore, but it was sweet of Polly to be so cooperative. Charlotte just assumed she'd be much more territorial.

"You were saying," Damen said, easing his hand off the silencer and clearing his throat. "Something about your boyfriend?"

"He is a great guy," Anais said, her mood turning suddenly sunnier. "But I don't think he really appreciates me."

"What makes you say that?" Damen asked, his curiosity piqued.

"I don't feel like he likes me for me," she informed. "Like maybe he wants me to be something I'm not."

"Did he ask you to change?" Damen asked.

"No," she said. "But he didn't *not* ask me."

That was a pretty wacky way to put it, Damen thought.

"Then maybe it's all in your head?" he responded dismissively. "Just some insecurities coming out."

No, he did not just tell a girl it was all in her head! Charlotte was desperate to get through, but she was getting nowhere. It was like dancing with a guy who knows only one step. So, she decided to take the lead.

"You are not hearing me," she said. "If it's real to me, then it's real."

Damen was stung and tried to process what she was saying. He was kind of literal in his approach to girls and relationships. Things were either good or bad, true or false; gray area

was not his specialty. He tried to find an example from his own life that would suit the situation.

"I once knew a girl that tried to change everything about herself," Damen offered. "And it really didn't go well."

"So?" Anais said, not sure where this was going.

"So, nobody asked her to change," Damen said. "She was smart, sweet, and helpful."

"*Helpful?*" Charlotte quizzed, putting a little more of herself into the chat. "You make her sound like a pet or something."

All she could think at the moment was that he left out "pretty." This was starting to get personal.

"My point is," Damen said, "she was fine exactly as she was."

"Maybe she didn't see it that way," she said defensively. "You can't tell someone else how to feel."

"True," Damen argued, "but you can't blame someone else for the way you feel or the choices you make either."

"Nobody makes decisions in a vacuum," Anais spouted, even more of Charlotte sneaking out of her mouth. "We can only react to the way people think about us."

"You can never really know what another person intends," Damen suggested, mining his recollection of first-semester ethical philosophy. "It's easy to get it wrong."

"So this girl you knew just imagined all of it?" Charlotte prodded.

"No," Damen continued, "but there was a big gap between reality and her perception of it."

"And she fell into the gap?" she said.

"It's not hard to do," Damen explained.

Charlotte was both flattered and flustered that he thought to use her as a talking point, but his analysis was colored by a whole lot of hindsight. Sure, nobody asked her to change. Nobody noticed her enough to bother. This conversation was bringing up a lot of long-buried, so to speak, bad memories.

"People expect you to be a certain way," she said, "to look a certain way, think a certain way. Otherwise they won't accept you."

"Then they're not worth impressing," Damen said easily. "Anyone who really cared about you wouldn't expect you to change for them."

"Easy for you to say," Charlotte let slip. "You have everything you want, great looks, great body, great girlfriend, great T-shirt."

Damen looked around, feeling as if he was being watched. What did this caller know about him or his life? Charlotte could see his distress.

"Do I know you?" Damen said.

"You must have it all figured out," she said, ignoring his question. "After all, you're on the radio."

"I don't have anything figured out, for myself or anyone else," Damen went on. "But, my guess is that your boyfriend loves you just the way you are. Thank you for your call."

Damen was dripping with sweat as he hung up the phone. He wondered if he'd been a little smug with the caller. More importantly, he wondered if he'd been a little smug with Scarlet lately.

Charlotte was not quite sure how she felt about the call either. This was the first real conversation she'd ever had with

Damen. It left her feeling good about him—she'd clearly been right about his innate steadiness, loyalty, and common sense—but melancholy about all those changes she'd made. Maybe she could have gotten him on her own merits after all. And *lived* happily ever after. Hopefully, Anais wouldn't make the same mistakes.

The real takeaway, she thought—the thing she was sure of—was that Damen loved Scarlet just the way she was. The problem was getting Scarlet to believe it.

Chapter 15

Secret Girls

I was feeling insecure
You might not love me anymore
—John Lennon

Tell-all.

---◆◆◆◆◆---

Sometimes divulging your vulnerabilities without any kind of filter can make you more human, but then again, it can also provide material that can be used against you. When you enter into a relationship, you want to know that person, every single detail, and you want them to know about you. You are an open book. But, if things don't work out, you better be prepared to duck when that same book is thrown back at you.

t was obvious from the second they pulled into the school parking lot that things had changed. Wendy Anderson and Wendy Thomas made the turn into the student entrance, and the early morning crowd parted, observing the invisible social barrier that separated them, to let them through. It wasn't just underclassmen; it was their peers, seniors, who were admiring them. At first, they just thought that everyone assumed Petula was with them, but as they made their way around the lot in Wendy Anderson's vintage MG Sprite convertible, it was obvious that wasn't the case.

Once they came around to the perfect spot, right in front of the sidewalk to the gym entrance, they saw Darcy waving them in. They realized then that they not only had her to thank for their good parking karma, but for their newfound

fame—the fame that they deserved but had never found, the fame that Petula had kept them from, and kept from them.

"I am getting dresses sent to me from everywhere. I haven't even gone through the boxes," Wendy Anderson said.

They both knew she was lying, but it was okay because they weren't about reality anymore. They were about perpetuating the image they worked so hard to project. They were a team, now more than ever, and they had a new leader in Darcy. The Wendys felt like shareholders in a corporation now, instead of just trophy friends.

"I have holds at three boutiques," Wendy Anderson said in a heated prom dress discussion. "I just can't make up my mind."

"You shouldn't let anyone know which dress you pick until that night," Wendy Thomas chirped.

"I'm actually thinking about wearing all three if I can reserve a quick change room," Wendy Anderson said. "Just keep it on the down-low for the media."

"Speaking of down-low," Wendy Thomas giggled.

The conversation turned from gowns to scowls as Petula pulled into the lot. As she exited the vehicle, a bag of give-aways rolled out with her, falling onto the pavement below and prompting chuckles from the stragglers doing their best to be late for class. She picked them up just as she would a tampon that fell out of her purse: quickly.

Watching Petula scurry to scoop up the clothing, the Wendys felt a twinge of guilt until Darcy arrived to put it in perspective for them.

"How selfish," Darcy said snidely, appearing from behind

The Wendys and draping her long, lean arms around their necks. "Airing her dirty laundry in public like that."

"That's not her laundry," Wendy Thomas corrected, staring blankly at the bag.

"Yeah," Wendy Anderson concurred, recalling Petula's germophobic repulsion toward public washers and dryers. "She limits her wardrobe to hand-washables and dry-clean-only."

Darcy was impressed with both how observant and how stupid they were.

"She has no idea how this reflects on both of you," Darcy continued to needle, shaking her head dejectedly to emphasize her point. The Wendys, clinging to Darcy like two parasites in need of a new host, nodded their brunette updos in agreement.

Scarlet raced into the parking lot as usual and spied the last empty spot a few spaces from Petula. As she pulled in, she could see Petula pick up the last few items that had fallen from her car, toss them in her backseat, and trudge off, head down, toward the front doors. In all her life, Scarlet couldn't recall ever having seen Petula hang her head.

Could this get any worse? Scarlet wondered as she saw the Wendys and Darcy leading the laughter. She was then slapped with an unequivocal "yes" as Petula was approached by a freshman wearing a handmade tee that had BANDTARD painted across the chest. He was obviously in the midst of being initiated and she was obviously being pranked.

Scarlet actually felt sorry for Petula as she witnessed her comeuppance. She'd gone from popular to punchline just like

that. The guy's voice was so inappropriately loud it was impossible not to hear him, even from this distance.

"Hey, I heard you need a date for prom," the freshman said, blocking her path, saliva unwittingly spraying from his mouth and onto her outfit as he stuttered out the invite.

"Ewww, cobra mouth," Darcy shouted.

Petula looked over and saw the Wendys and Darcy hunched over the hood of their car, laughing like rabid, über-fashionable hyenas. The bandtard came over to them with his hand out, and Darcy peeled off a few singles and thanked him.

"That was cheap," Darcy chuckled to The Wendys.

"You should know," Scarlet swiped as she approached, getting in all their faces.

"What comes around goes around," Wendy Anderson said.

"Just like an STD," Scarlet punched back. "Ain't that right, Wendy?"

Wendy Anderson clammed up immediately, and Wendy Thomas wasn't about to jump in.

"I'd really love to get into a battle of wits with you guys, but I never attack anyone unarmed," Scarlet said, silencing The Wendys' hope for retaliation.

"Hey, maybe you can go with that bandtard if Petula passes," Darcy said, offering her a few bucks. "I hear *you* might need a date."

⊛⊗

The song contest was picking up steam, and the radio station phone lines started lighting up like crazy.

"Look at that," Damen said, studying his computer screen, as Scarlet's song topped the voter list. "I think we have a hit on our hands."

He said "we" instead of "she" because he really considered it their song. She'd written the lyrics for him, but he'd laid down a smoking-hot guitar track on it.

Wait until I tell Scarlet! he thought, and then remembered that she wasn't too happy he'd submitted the song in the first place.

Charlotte watched helplessly as his mood changed. There was a sadness in his eyes that she'd never seen before. The optimism, confidence, and determination that everyone admired about him were giving way to self-doubt and uncertainty.

"Don't worry," Charlotte said as she moved around behind his chair and placed her hands gently on his shoulders. "Scarlet will see that you're doing all this for her," she whispered in his ear.

His neck and shoulders relaxed as he eased back into the chair. Charlotte was here to help him, and she felt that she had begun to do her part, however small, to comfort him.

Seeing the phones lighting up in support of Scarlet made him feel especially close to her, so he pulled out his letter, determined to finish it up.

Charlotte read over his shoulder as he collected his thoughts and copied them down. Finally satisfied that he'd said all he meant to say, Damen closed the letter, as he always did, with a "Y.T.N.F." and pulled back to read the valediction aloud before he signed it.

"Yours…Till…Niagara…Falls, Damen."

Charlotte swooned. She would have died to hear something like that from Eric, or anybody for that matter. It was corny, sure, but Charlotte was a sucker for that kind of thing. The thought of roaring white water rolling endlessly over rocky cliffs to the riverbed below conjured up images of infinite, undying, ever-renewing love.

Just then the program director, Jerry Stylus, burst in the room.

"Dylan!" the PD barked. "Did you submit this track?"

"Yep," Damen answered proudly, gesturing to the call-in board. "It's absolutely killing!"

"Maybe so," Stylus acknowledged, "but unfortunately, it's my turn to do some killing. The song is disqualified."

Charlotte gulped so loudly she feared they might hear her.

"No way!" Damen yelled, jumping to his feet.

Charlotte had never seen him in such a state. It was as if Scarlet was standing right there beside him and had been insulted personally.

Mr. Stylus quickly realized he shouldn't have been so cavalier. He waved the cue sheet for the song up and over the console, close enough for him to read to Damen, but not so close that he might get punched out.

"I was just reviewing the credits for all the submissions, and I see you did the music on the track."

"Yeah, so?" Damen was pacing behind his chair and trying desperately to calm himself. "It's my girlfriend's song."

"It's against the rules," Stylus informed him. "No station employee can participate in any on-air contest."

"So, you mean if I hadn't taken this job…" Damen's voice trailed off.

Charlotte knew what he really meant to say. If he hadn't come home, if he hadn't changed everything to be near her, none of this would have happened. It was a series of unintended consequences that he'd set in motion. He only meant to be with her and to show his love and support by recording her song and submitting it. And now it had all gone wrong.

"It's standard conflict-of-interest stuff," Jerry concluded as he folded up the cue sheet and handed it tentatively to Damen. "Sorry, kid."

"Sorry?" Damen said sarcastically, dropping down in his seat and hanging his head. "You're not the only one."

This was going to be a problem. Scarlet never wanted to be entered to begin with, but now that she was, Damen knew she was excited about it, even though she'd never admit it to him. She was going to be shattered by the disqualification, and so would their relationship.

"If you don't mind," Stylus requested, adding insult to injury, "just delete the track from the playlist before the end of your shift."

Damen nodded silently.

"Niagara…," Charlotte mouthed somberly, "falls."

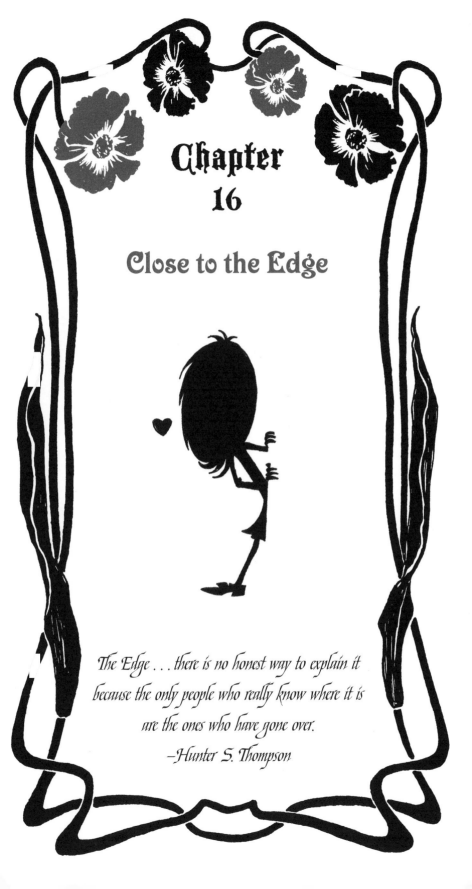

Chapter
16

Close to the Edge

The Edge . . . there is no honest way to explain it because the only people who really know where it is are the ones who have gone over.
—Hunter S. Thompson

Love is a drug.

———◆◈◆———

Falling in love is transformational but not always in the ways that we hope. You go from being a whole person to being half a relationship, sometimes losing a large part of yourself in the process. Unfortunately, it is almost always the secure, self-assured part of you that turns up missing. But the real trouble begins when you need another person to help you find it.

**ey," Charlotte said as she approached** Eric, who was hanging out on the front steps of IdentiTea, fiddling with his guitar. He looked a little like a puppy waiting for its master, a far cry from the street-tough punk she knew and, although she hadn't said it yet, loved.

"Hey," Eric replied, looking up at her with some excitement, but then immediately putting his head back down to continue playing.

"I'm here," Charlotte responded.

"So I see," Eric said.

It was oddly strained and awkward between them, leaving Charlotte more suspicious than ever about his feelings for Scarlet.

"So, what have you been up to?" Charlotte asked.

"Just hanging out," he said. "You?"

"Nothing much, just trying to help smooth things over," she said, watching his face for any reaction. "Damen loves her so much. You're never going to believe how he signs his letters to her."

"She isn't happy," Eric snapped.

"Why do you care so much if she's happy?" Charlotte asked pointedly.

What she wanted to say was, why don't you care about *my* being happy, but she fought the urge.

"Because that's why I'm here," Eric said defensively.

"Are you sure about that?" Charlotte asked.

"What are you trying to get at, Charlotte?"

"I think you'd better check your motives," she said, her jealousy no longer remotely veiled.

"I think you'd better check yourself," Eric said as Damen passed them and went into the café. "Frankly, I don't really care what he writes to her in letters."

"Oh, I forgot," Charlotte snapped, "it's not *cool* to express your feelings like that, is it?"

Eric put his guitar down and looked Charlotte in the eyes.

"Why are you always so quick to point out how inadequate I am?"

"I didn't mean it that way," Charlotte said, extending her neck a bit to see what was happening inside.

"What way did you mean it, then?" Eric asked, annoyed that she was suddenly distracted by Damen's arrival.

"We're here to do a job, for them, not for us," Charlotte said, refocusing on Eric.

"That's my point, exactly," he said. "I am thinking about her, but it seems you might be thinking of yourself first."

"What are you talking about?"

"You know what I'm talking about."

"Are you trying to say that I'm pushing Damen to get back with Scarlet because I'm jealous of her being with you?"

"You're the one who said it."

"Can you get over yourself for just a second?" Charlotte asked as she watched him strum away.

She put her hand on the neck of the guitar and held the strings so he couldn't play.

"Look at me!" Charlotte ordered, becoming increasingly upset.

Their first-ever fight was officially on before they'd even had their first kiss.

"You're going to make a scene."

"Are you hushing me?"

"No, just cool it a little."

Charlotte began to tremble.

"Make a scene?" she said. "No one could possibly see us except Scarlet."

Charlotte knew from the look on his face that that's exactly what he was worried about. His follow-up was even more telling.

"Did it ever occur to you," Eric suggested, "that we might be here to keep them apart?"

৩৩

Damen arrived at IdentiTea looking for Scarlet but found The Wendys and Darcy instead.

"Hey, Damen, what's up?" Wendy Anderson greeted him cordially.

"Here to see your girlfriend?" Wendy Thomas added before Damen could answer. "You just missed her."

Damen wasn't surprised. He and Scarlet had been missing each other in every way for a while. The Wendys sensed Damen's urgency and physically blocked him from getting through to guarantee a little face time.

"She *is* still your girlfriend, isn't she?" Wendy Thomas gibed.

"Why wouldn't she be?" Damen asked snidely, not wanting to throw even the tiniest piece of red meat to Hawthorne's voracious gossips.

"Oh, we just heard some stuff," Wendy Anderson said.

"From who?" Damen asked. "Scarlet?"

"Oh, no, no," Darcy interjected. "Not from her."

"Who are *you*?" Damen asked. "And what the hell are you doing in my business?"

"This is Darcy," Wendy Thomas said. "She's new."

"I've heard a lot about you," Darcy cooed, snuggling up to Damen as if they were the only two in the room.

As this was unfolding, Eric walked over to Scarlet.

"Hey, Scarlet, I'm gonna catch you later," he said.

"So soon?" Scarlet asked.

"I love this place, but it gets boring here sometimes."

"You won't be bored. You've got company," she said, grabbing her bag.

As they walked away, Charlotte saw Eric pointing Scarlet in Damen's and Darcy's direction. It was as if he wanted Damen to get caught talking to another girl. Like he was working against her. Or more like, against Damen.

Or maybe he was just working for Scarlet.

Damen wasn't quite sure how to approach Scarlet about the disqualification. Long story short, she was going to be mad. If he was too morose, she might assume he was feeling guilty and looking for sympathy from her when she was the one who actually needed the support. Maybe, he thought, the best way to deal with it was offhandedly. Scarlet might even be relieved to be out of the running for a competition she'd never intended to enter.

He braced himself as he walked up to her front door, hoping he'd picked the right approach.

"Hey," Damen said, "I've got some great news."

"What's that," Scarlet mumbled, barely acknowledging him. He followed her up to her room.

"Your song," Damen began.

"What now?" Scarlet cut him off. "Did you get an offer from a record label?"

"Not exactly." Damen paused, swallowing hard. "It was disqualified."

Scarlet looked up at him from her bed and remained silent for a few seconds, not quite sure if she'd heard him right.

"What?" she screamed.

From her tone, he guessed relief was not exactly the emotion she was feeling.

"Employees of the station can't enter contests," Damen explained calmly as she stared him down scornfully. "I'm sorry."

"So it's all your fault?" Scarlet exploded, his apology clearly not enough for her.

This was the Scarlet he'd known when he was dating Petula

and hadn't seen since then. Tough, outspoken, brutal. Any worries she had about losing her true self were definitely misplaced, he thought.

"That's not fair," Damen countered, trying hard not to lose his temper. "I had no idea."

"Not fair to whom?" She went on, "I didn't ask to be entered but I'm the big loser anyway."

"*We* lost," Damen attempted to remind her.

"*I* lost," Scarlet barked spitefully. "It was my name on the song, not yours."

"Right," Damen shot back reflexively. "It wasn't my name, just my guitar."

Damen instantly realized that he might have picked at a scab that was a little too fresh. Scarlet knew she was no guitar god; that was part of the reason she hadn't submitted the song herself. She didn't have enough confidence in her ability, Eric's compliments notwithstanding.

The fact that Damen, however unwittingly, just called her out on it really hurt. He knew her weaknesses and he should have known better than to expose them, no matter how angry she made him. Maybe, she thought, he *did* know better and was finally being honest.

"I guess I'm just not good enough," Scarlet exhaled. "For you."

Her comment spoke volumes. It wasn't about the song at all. It was about everything else. The way she looked, the way she dressed, the things she liked or didn't. None of it was good enough for him. At least that's how she'd been feeling, and now she'd said it.

He moved in to hug her, but she tightened up and turned away.

Frustrated with her and with himself, he decided he'd had enough.

"I don't think this is working," Damen said. "Maybe we shouldn't be together after all."

Scarlet was surprised at how much hearing him say that hurt. She'd been pretty much pushing him in that direction, but now that he was the one to say it, to make it real, it broke her heart.

"Why don't you go back where you belong," Scarlet said. "And I'll stay where I belong."

Where exactly she meant, Damen didn't have a clue. Back to work, back to college, or back to his life before her? Maybe all of the above.

"Yeah, maybe you're right," he said, stunning her even further. "Maybe I just don't belong with you."

She thought they might not be good for each other, but deep down she just wanted him to convince her that they were, like he always had before.

"Here, here's a note that I wrote to you explaining things," he said, handing her the piece of paper he had slaved over. "You can read it or not. It's up to you," he mumbled as he walked away.

Scarlet took the note out of his hand, stared at it, and then set it on the nightstand, next to her belongings. And there it stayed—unread.

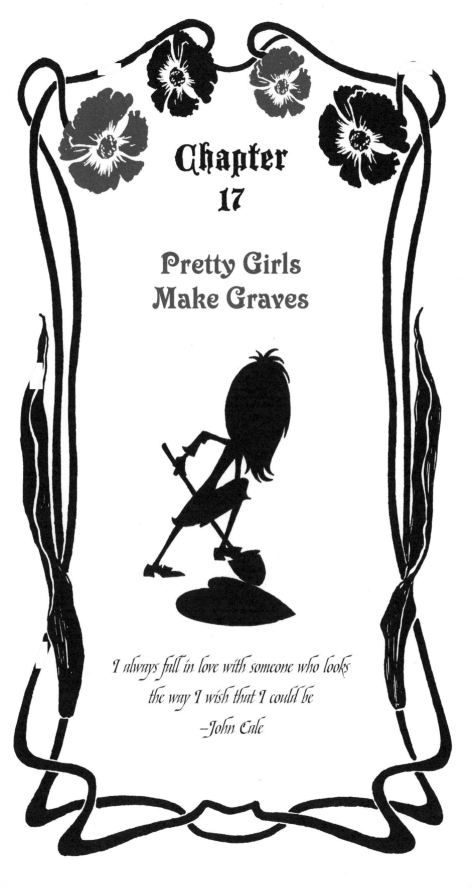

Chapter 17

Pretty Girls
Make Graves

*I always fall in love with someone who looks
the way I wish that I could be
—John Cale*

Final exam.

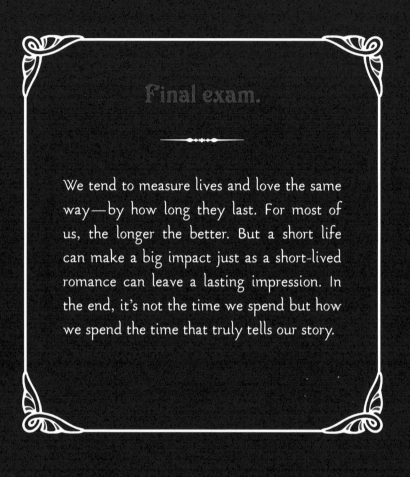

We tend to measure lives and love the same way—by how long they last. For most of us, the longer the better. But a short life can make a big impact just as a short-lived romance can leave a lasting impression. In the end, it's not the time we spend but how we spend the time that truly tells our story.

etula thought that maybe once she got really into it, her excitement, her rush would kick in, but as of this moment, she wasn't really feeling it. CoCo had done her best to rummage through the piles, assembling beautifully color-coordinated combinations for Petula to stumble upon. Any top fashion editor would spontaneously combust at the sight of these outfits, but they didn't even rug-shock Petula.

For the first time, she didn't notice colors or cuts. She felt as if nothing mattered anymore. Her life was over. So maybe The Wendys were right; maybe she was crazy. The only compulsion she was feeling now was to pull up a cardboard box and catnap on the curb.

Just like the destitute she had inexplicably committed to serve, Petula was an outcast. Shunned. All that she had strived to be was now undone, and despite all the blatant paranoia exhibited by The Wendys and the plotting by Darcy, it was her own fault. This was particularly distressing for Petula since up until now, the only purpose for a good, hard look in the mirror had been to check for flyaways. After all, it was much easier, she was learning, to assign blame than to assume it.

In the end, she reckoned, popularity was a temporary condition—a virus that bounces like the flu bug, predominantly

to those made susceptible by their winning gene pools. The strength of each strain is determined by the insecurity, desperation, and sheer number of those hoping to acquire it.

Petula figured that was why high school lasted only four years, maybe five, in her case. Popularity fatigue, even immunity, was bound to set in among the masses after that. All this philosophizing and self-recrimination was making her head hurt, and Petula wanted to call it a day. She wanted to get back in her car, go home, and beg for her old life back. But, something, or someone, wasn't letting her.

CoCo didn't really care much about helping the needy, or Petula for that matter. But she did care a lot about clothes, and she was the first to realize that overthrowing Petula was just a smoke screen for Darcy. Her real goal, CoCo surmised, was to demoralize Petula into giving up her fashion moonlighting altogether, leaving the destitute to their understyled and hopeless existence. CoCo was literally providing moral support to keep that from happening. On a scale of global problems, it was a very minor affair, but any increase in the misery index, CoCo felt, must be fought. This, after all, was Markov's point.

In almost a stupor, Petula grabbed some men's outfits and hit the streets once again, with CoCo trailing close behind. As she drove them down to the dreary destination, she continued to berate herself out loud, beating herself up emotionally. Petula was fine with change, as long as it was of the cosmetic variety. Tampering with whatever was on the inside had been strictly forbidden. Until recently.

Petula double-parked, picked up her sack of clothing, and headed for the nearest corrugated shanty. She wasn't being

lazy. CoCo had seen something, actually *someone*, at that location who'd caught her attention on her last few visits, and she was determined to guide Petula there. As they drew nearer, Petula noticed a rustling under the garbage-festooned box and heard a few loud grunts. She had yet to see any definite proof that the source of the movement was human, but she was strangely unafraid. She felt protected.

"Hello?" Petula said.

No one answered her.

"Hey!" Petula screeched, kicking at the box and demanding to be charitable.

"What do you want?" the heap said in a grouchy voice.

It was definitely a male voice.

"Now, that's a good question, one that I've been asking myself over and over again for the past few months," she said. "What about you? What do you want?"

The homeless person started breaking out of his handout-clothing cocoon.

"I want to be left alone," he muttered while freeing himself from the poly-blend cloaking his head. "Not dragged into your internal monologue."

As the clothes fell away from his face, his eyes met with Petula's. They were crystal blue and Petula couldn't help but swim in them.

"You're...," she began, "young."

"There's no age requirement for being homeless, as far as I know," he said.

He looked more movie-set dirty than filthy, Petula observed, as if some makeup assistant, rather than a hard-knock life, had

dusted him down. CoCo stood and stared proudly as a look of accomplishment washed over her face.

"What are you doing here?" she asked. "You don't really look like you belong."

"I should ask you the same," he replied.

She didn't really have an answer for him, and so she never got one from him.

"We must be around the same age," she said.

"Yeah, we've got that in common," he said.

"I'm sure we have more than just that in common," Petula said.

"Yeah, like what?"

"We both worry about clothes," she said, thinking fast. "I worry that I have the latest and the hottest pieces, and you, well, you worry that you have…any."

"I guess that's something," he said, smiling slightly.

"Hey, your teeth are really white," she said, taken aback by his shiny grin. "Like, professional white."

The guy looked more than embarrassed by the compliment.

One thing about homeless people that was hard for Petula to take was their lack of dental hygiene, and there was nothing Petula hated more than butterteeth. She even kept a Baggie of whitening strips and travel-size toothbrushes in her purse to help them combat their fuzzy tooth sweaters.

"These are for you," Petula said, eyeing him as she handed over the jackets, shirts, and suit pants she'd pilfered from her guest-room closet. "I think they'll fit."

Petula didn't just think it; she knew it. She was an expert at evaluating body types.

"Thanks," he said shyly, as if he were taking something he didn't deserve. "Now if you'll excuse me."

Just as he began to limp away Petula called out to him.

"I'm Petula, by the way," she said, pursing her lips and quickly slipping on a latex surgical glove as she thrust her hand outward to greet him.

"Tate," he said, grabbing her forearm and squeezing. "Nice to meet you."

Petula saw that he wasn't actually hurt. He was faking his limp. She could tell because she'd "come down" with homeless-leg syndrome occasionally herself whenever she exited her car in a handicapped space at the mall. Between his faux gimp and the pearly whites, Petula thought something didn't quite compute.

As she watched them say their awkward goodbyes and Petula started back to her car, CoCo was startled by the pay phone ringing behind her. She looked around to see if any-one else heard it, but then noticed the out-of-order sticker on the dial. She decided it could only be for her. Ever the neat and clean freak, she balked at touching the receiver and instinctively used the cuff of her sleeve to cover her hand as she picked up the phone. CoCo was a creature of habit and death had changed very little for her.

"Showroom," CoCo answered firmly.

"CoCo, it's Gary."

"I'm just in the middle of something, darling," CoCo said hurriedly. "Can I get right back to you?"

"You are wanted at the office," he advised.

"But what about Petula?" CoCo began to ask.

The click in her ear signaled the end of the connection

and the conversation. CoCo watched in frustration as Petula headed toward her car and sped off, slowly fading from view.

❦

Charlotte was looking for a way out, literally. She headed to Hawthorne and the intake office with Pam and Prue following behind anxiously. The last time she was here it was to save Petula. This time, Charlotte thought, it was to save herself.

"I'm going back," Charlotte said as she grabbed for the office door.

"What do you mean you're going back?" Pam asked, using her foot as a doorstopper.

"You can't go back until you're called," Prue added.

"Everything is going wrong," Charlotte said. "There's no point staying."

"But that's why we're here," Pam scolded. "To make things better."

"We're making things worse," Charlotte argued. "For the living and ourselves! Maybe we failed."

Pam and Prue didn't respond. It was something they'd been thinking, as well, but were not quite willing to admit.

"Don't be so self-absorbed," Prue finally shot back. "Just because you and Eric might not work out, doesn't mean that nothing here will."

Charlotte bristled at the criticism, not just because she was angry with her friends, but because they had a point. Being back always brought out the pessimist in her, and this time was no exception.

"It's not just about me and Eric," Charlotte said. "Everyone is lonely and miserable, except, of course, The Wendys."

"What's that supposed to mean?" Pam asked.

"It means that the two people who deserve happiness the least are getting exactly what they always wanted," Charlotte scolded. "Nice work."

"That's not fair, Charlotte," Pam said. "We're all trying."

"As long as we're here, there's still work to be done," Prue said, frustrated. "Get a grip."

"Okay, I will," Charlotte said, gripping the door handle. "Get out of my way."

Pam stood aside and the door opened. It was the same as it was the first day she arrived there. Cold and spare. She made her way to the counter and took a number. There was the same secretary, the one who didn't look up, sitting behind the desk in her same funeral home attire with the casket-ready ruffled blouse Charlotte wouldn't have been caught dead or alive wearing.

"Sit down and I'll call your name," she said.

Charlotte was tempted to say hello, but the secretary didn't seem to recognize her. Not surprising, Charlotte thought, since she processed so many souls.

"We can't let you do this," Pam argued. "It's just not right."

"It is right for me," Charlotte insisted.

The threesome continued their argument as they walked over to the bench, oblivious to the fact that there was someone else in the room. A girl, nervous and coiled up in the corner.

"They should really play better music in this place," Pam said, trying to make small talk.

The girl didn't look up. She was too afraid. They could certainly relate to that and put their differences aside for the moment to reach out to the new arrival. It looked to them as

if she'd been there for a while, though her name had not been called or a greeter assigned to escort her to the Dead Ed classroom. She seemed disoriented and very much out of place.

"Hi. I'm Charlotte," she said softly as she approached. "This is Prue and this is Pam."

"Do you know where you are?" Prue asked.

"Has anyone come for you?" Pam inquired further.

The girl shook her head "No" silently.

"What's your name?" Charlotte asked gently.

The girl looked up at them slowly. Her face was a familiar one. Prue and Pam's jaws dropped in shock. Charlotte's too. And for maybe the first time ever the three of them were speechless.

"I'm Darcy," she answered.

ॐ

Pam, Prue, and Charlotte quickly excused themselves and stepped outside the office.

"What the hell is going on here?" Prue asked in frustration.

"If that's Darcy in there," Pam continued, "Then who is that hanging out with The Wendys?"

"They're both Darcy," Charlotte said cryptically.

They were all thinking the same thing, but no one wanted to be the first to blurt it.

"What are we going to do about it?" Prue continued.

"What *can* we do?" Pam responded.

Before Charlotte could respond, the new Dead Ed classmates came walking toward them. Charlotte shushed Pam and Prue and signaled that they'd pick up the conversation later. They were struck by how young and naive the new girls appeared and realized they must have seemed the same back

then. It was funny, and a little bit sad as well, how much a little knowledge and experience could change you.

"Hi, Charlotte," Mercury Mary called out. "Remember us?"

"Sure, Mary," Charlotte said. "These are my friends Pam and Prue. Ladies, meet Mercury Mary, Toxic Shock Sally, and Scared to Beth. "

With the niceties out of the way, Charlotte hit on an idea.

"Hey, girls," Charlotte asked, "would you mind doing us a favor?"

"Nothing dangerous, is it?" Scared to Beth asked.

"Not at all," Charlotte said.

"Okay, then," Sally agreed, stifling her tremors for the moment.

"There is a girl named Darcy sitting in the office," Charlotte said. "She's a little lonely. Would you mind hanging out with her for a while?"

Pam and Prue instantly caught Charlotte's drift.

"Maybe find out more about her," Pam added. "You know, how she got here."

"No problem," Mary said eagerly, more than happy to help.

Mary, Sally, and Beth entered the office and closed the door behind them, leaving Pam, Prue, and Charlotte to finish their conversation.

"I have an idea," Charlotte whispered.

"Uh-oh," Pam teased.

She was worried Charlotte was about to turn from supernatural to super sleuth.

"In order to make things right," Charlotte explained, "we need to get Darcy out of the picture."

"But to do that…," Pam prompted.

"Darcy must die," Charlotte said.

Chapter 18

I Know You by Heart

How will you know if you found me at last
'cause I'll be the one with my heart in my lap.
—Neko Case

Love song.

————◆━◆◆━◆————

Like a tune that you can't get out of your
head no matter how hard you try, love is
something you can't get out of your heart. You
become trapped in an emotional cul de sac,
going round and round and ending up exactly
where you started. Breaking free, or not, is
usually determined by whether you want to
get somewhere slowly or nowhere fast.

**carlet loved to hang out at Vinyl** Frontier, a used-record store she frequented. It used to be called Permanent Records until it burned down and was rebuilt. It was a little hole-in-the-wall place, but it was a place where she could spend hours listening to any record she wanted without having to buy anything. The owner, Mr. Hood, was a cool guy who taught English lit at her school. He was a closet musician who played local clubs and considered teaching his day job. He used to sleep the last ten minutes of each class and say that if he got that time, he didn't need to sleep at night.

Scarlet liked being at Vinyl Frontier for the same reason she liked scrounging through thrift stores and even visiting the cemetery. There was so much life to be found among forgotten things. In fact, if she wanted to, she could take her fingernail or the pin from her brooch and place it gently in the

grooves and with a few careful spins, resurrect all the passion, energy, and magic that had created it. Try doing *that* on your touch screen, she thought.

Hood liked Scarlet. Whenever she paid a visit, word would get out, upping the store's hip factor and, consequently, his sales. It was like a celebrity in-store appearance, so he didn't mind giving her free run of the place after hours. It was a fair trade. That, and the fact that Scarlet wasn't some stupid kid; she was a music historian, a true music lover. She knew her stuff—from the classics all the way to the most esoteric. They had many a late-night discussion about all the different genres of music, but mostly they didn't talk, they just listened.

She shared with him not just a love of the sound of an analog recording playing back but a devotion to the actual platters and square cardboard album jackets themselves. Compared to the digital liner notes that were now offered for download, they seemed like museum-quality artwork.

The thing about records, Scarlet felt, was the physical relationship they created to the music. Unlike CDs or computer files, vinyl was fragile, easily damaged, and hard to replace. It needed to be cared for, respected, and protected from harm. She could relate.

Hood also explained a little to her about the business side of music, knowing she might have some aspirations in that regard. He told her how so few artists made money from records, even if they sold well. There was something called "breakage" deducted from an artist's royalties that literally

took into account that a certain percentage of vinyl albums were likely to be damaged in shipping to shops like his. She was fascinated by the concept, by the fact that "damage" was anticipated. Maybe that was the way people should enter relationships, she thought.

It was so common-sensible. Nothing lasts forever, she thought: albums, people, or even relationships, especially if they aren't handled with care. The other side, of course, was that the scratches and chips that were cut into the grooves were proof that the disc had been played. It made them a record, not just of someone's music, but of someone listening to it.

Lately, Scarlet found herself being drawn to songs about loneliness and heartbreak. It was obvious that she missed Damen, but she felt that their separation was for the best. Things take time. She knew that, and with time and some really good music, she would heal. She listened intently with the oversize headphones cementing her black hair to her ivory skin. The music began to fade and then out of nowhere, blasted in her ear.

"What the…?" she screeched angrily, pulling the headphones out a few inches.

Mr. Hood was sitting behind the register gathering his things, getting ready to close up.

Scarlet went back to listening, and no sooner did she get back into the song than it happened again. She looked around and past the displays into the back room where Mr. Hood and his band would practice. It was a raw, loftlike space

packed with instruments and amps. She saw Eric standing there, laughing and looking totally at home. She didn't want to alert Mr. Hood, for fear she would get Eric in trouble, so she excused herself to go use the restroom.

"Hey," Mr. Hood said. "I'm going to head out."

"Okay, I'll lock up," she said.

"I trust you," he said as he shut the door and locked it behind him.

Scarlet felt a little uneasy but not enough to leave.

"What are you doing here?" she asked Eric curiously. "I'm not allowed to have friends here after hours."

"I was walking past and I saw you in the window," he said. "Just thought I'd drop by and say 'hey.'"

"You could use the front door," she said.

"Too predictable."

Scarlet started fiddling with one of the guitars, fingering the chords to one of her songs.

"What's that?"

"Oh, nothing, just some stupid song I wrote," she said.

"Sounds cool to me," he said.

"Actually, it was entered into this radio contest, but it got disqualified 'cause of a conflict of interest," she said, not wanting to get too deep into the details. "My boyfriend entered it, but he works at the station, so..."

Eric got it. It clearly meant a lot to her to have her song in the contest, and she wanted it to be heard. He could appreciate her disappointment.

"There's always a conflict," he said vaguely.

"What do you mean?" Scarlet asked, thinking her situation was pretty unusual.

"Between guys and girls."

She smiled, knowing exactly what he meant.

"I wrote this song for a girl I was really into, but we split up before I ever had a chance to play it for her," he said as he strummed the first few chords.

"That's beautiful." Scarlet nodded along. "She must have meant a lot to you."

"Still does," Eric added, still playing.

"I hear you," she said, simply swaying to the beat, feeling his music and his emotions too.

"My dream was to perform in front of a crowd," Eric said to Scarlet, the disappointment in his voice contrasting with the joy in his music. "But right now, all I want to do is play this for her."

"It's never too late," she replied. "I learned that from a very good friend of mine."

As Eric continued to play, Scarlet began humming a melody line and a few words and phrases over it. Scarlet saw a softer side of Eric that she hadn't seen before. She was staring at him but thinking of Damen as the verses for a new song came to her. If she didn't know better, she might have thought Eric had planned it that way. As he ended the song, Eric made an enthusiastic pitch that he thought might be good for both of them.

"Maybe we can work on something together," he suggested. "You know, collaborate."

Scarlet wasn't sure if asking to "collaborate" was his way of hitting on her. She hoped not, but it reminded her that they were virtual strangers all alone together in the back room of a locked-up record shop. She didn't want to end up on the evening news, but at the same time, she felt close to him. Spiritually, more than anything else.

"I don't think I'm ready," she said, hoping to answer several questions, asked or not, with a single sound bite. "But if I was going to collaborate with somebody, it would be you."

"I just thought that maybe they'd let you replace your old song in the competition." Eric pulled back a little, thinking he might have come on a little strong. "I bet your boyfriend would like that."

"He's not my boyfriend," she said, escorting Eric out of the store, "anymore."

⯎

Mary, Beth, and Sally stepped out of the intake office to be debriefed about Darcy.

"She has no idea where she is," Mary began, "or why she's there."

"That's not news," Prue said, showing her usual impatience with underclassmen. "Nobody ever does."

"Did she tell you the last thing she remembered doing?" Pam asked, more calmly.

"She said she was taking some glamour shots for the Gorey High yearbook," Sally added, "but that's all."

It took her a second, but Charlotte figured it out. She'd

been a pretty avid picture taker when she was alive, mostly of Damen, granted, but in her studies she'd come across a few cases of people who were prone to epileptic fits from a flash-gun. That's one of the reasons why she always adhered to the rock-star rule of no flash photography in the stage pit. That, and the fact that it was much more difficult to sneak a picture of someone across the room with a strobe popping.

"She must have had a seizure," Charlotte surmised. "A really bad one."

"How do you know?" Beth asked, a shiver of fear in her voice.

"Some people react that way to flashbulbs," Prue jumped in. "Photosensitivity."

"Not just the flickering light," Charlotte expounded, "but the stress hormones from the pressure to look beautiful can push you right over the edge."

"If it was bad enough to almost kill her," Pam continued, "her soul might have disengaged from her body."

"Like Petula when she went into her coma," Charlotte agreed. "Except Darcy was probably revived much sooner."

"But there would still be enough time for someone or some-thing with bad intentions to get in there," Pam said.

"Someone?" Mary asked, confused like the rest of her class-mates. "Who would want to do that?"

Charlotte, Pam, and Prue just stared at each other and let the question go for the moment and got busy.

"We're going to need everyone's help," Charlotte pressed on, "here at the office and at prom."

"Prom?" Prue groused. "Is this *your* way of getting there?"

Charlotte was a little hurt.

"It's not like you have the best track record," Pam said out of the side of her mouth to Charlotte.

"No, it's my way of getting Damen there," Charlotte answered cryptically.

"See what I mean!" Prue cried, throwing up her hands. "Now that we're back here, it's 'Eric *who*?'"

"You mean Darcy, don't you?" Pam corrected, shushing Prue.

"I mean both of them," Charlotte responded. "Together."

Pam and Prue weren't quite sure where she was going, and the Dead Ed girls had no idea about Damen or prom, but Charlotte was persuasive enough that they were all willing to go along for the ride. Again.

೧೦

Scarlet arrived home from the record store to an unusual sight: her mom sitting up in the kitchen nursing a cup of tea and looking worried. What should have been a fairly relaxing event seemed anything but to Scarlet, and she spoke up.

"Mom?" Scarlet queried. "Anything wrong?"

"Have you spoken to your sister lately?" Kiki answered in an atypically cryptic manner.

"Not if I can help it," Scarlet said.

Despite the snarky attitude, Scarlet had been meaning to talk with Petula for a while now to show some solidarity in the face of The Wendys' mutiny. But commiserating with Petula was something she'd never done before, and taking the first step had

definitely proved to be challenging. Scarlet felt like a mosquito on a nude beach. She knew what to do but didn't know where to begin.

"She's got a lot going on," Kiki said, "and I'm worried she's not thinking clearly."

"Status quo," Scarlet said, shrugging.

"No attitude, please," her mom insisted. "This is serious."

"Serious how?" Scarlet asked with a bit more concern in her voice.

Maybe Petula had turned stripper—that would explain the late nights and rumors about her sister hanging out downtown. Keeping her off the pole had been a lifelong but so far unfounded worry of Kiki's. Or, Scarlet considered, Petula might have become an identity thief, picking through Dumpsters for credit card receipts. Scarlet quickly dismissed that notion. Petula, she knew with absolute certainty, would never want to be anyone else.

"She wants to ask a homeless guy to prom," Kiki announced.

Scarlet shuddered like she'd just been tasered by a policeman's stun gun.

"She needs someone to talk to," Kiki declared. "Do it for me."

Kiki had always respected her daughters' personality clash and never sought to force their relationship. So if she was asking Scarlet to reach out, it had to be really important to her.

Scarlet trudged up the stairs to Petula's room, not knowing what to say or expect. As she peeked in the door, Scarlet could

see Petula matching outfits, no longer hiding her causes. She was literally out of the closet now.

"What's up?" Scarlet said, gingerly stepping across the threshold and into Petula's sanctuary.

Scarlet looked around and could find few signs of Petula's once vaunted meticulousness. The room was a mess, strewn with clothes and accessories, drawers and closets half-open, and rumpled bedding. Like Petula, the surroundings just seemed wilted.

Scarlet jumped right in.

"We're all really proud of you for caring, but a homeless guy?" Scarlet asked, skeptically. "To prom?"

"I prefer to think of him as bohemian," Petula interrupted. "Besides, who are *you* going with?"

That kind of slam would usually be the end of any serious conversation between them, but Scarlet gritted her teeth and let it go, pressing on for her mother's sake.

"I'm just trying to understand what's going on with you," Scarlet prodded gently.

"He's different," Petula huffed. "And so am I. Just stay out of my business."

"It sucks what The Wendys and that other clone Darcy did to you," Scarlet offered sympathetically.

"I don't need your pity," Petula shot back, compulsively mixing and matching while she spoke. "I did what I did. No apologies."

"Okay," Scarlet said. "But what, exactly, did you do?"

The sisters stared at each other for a long while, Petula

searching futilely for a plausible answer. Suddenly, Petula cracked. Not a huge earthquake-size fault, but a tiny fissure, enough to let off the emotional and psychological steam that had been building inside her.

"I've been hanging out with the homeless people downtown," Petula wailed almost hysterically. "I've been giving them our old clothes."

This outburst was so unlike Petula, Scarlet had no idea who was in the room talking to her—maybe, she thought, a changeling or something.

"Why?" Scarlet asked, completely perplexed.

"I've been styling them," Petula confessed convulsively through her tears, as if she was vomiting up sins she'd been hiding her whole life. "I am becoming a, a…"

Petula could barely get the word out. Her tongue was swelling and her throat was closing up, as if she was choking on the very thought of the kindness she'd been showing.

"A humanitarian?" Scarlet suggested softly, putting up her hands like a boxer in case Petula took offense and lashed out.

"Yes!" Petula screamed in obvious pain, falling onto her bed and smashing her pillows over and over with clenched fists. "A crunchy, considerate, bleeding heart."

"That's not so bad," Scarlet said, awkwardly attempting to comfort her sister.

"Not so bad?" Petula spit. "I'm practically a hippie for God's sake!"

"Hardly," Scarlet thought, staring at the back of Petula's

waxed and perma-tanned legs, which ended right at her four-inch stilettos.

"My friends, my reputation, my *brand*," Petula moaned. "All gone."

"They aren't your friends," Scarlet said. "They're mercenaries."

Petula made a mental note that Scarlet left her reputation and brand worries unremarked upon.

"This is your way of removing the toxins from your life," Scarlet advised. "Like those alkaline drink and 'no-chewing' diets you torture yourself with."

"Maybe, but all I know is Hawthorne is going to have the best-dressed bums in the world," Petula said, "and I'm going to be fitted for a straitjacket and a pair of papier-mâché shower shoes."

"That might be a great new look for you," Scarlet laughed, getting a smile out of Petula as well.

"Life is not fair," Petula said finally after a long pause. "Not everyone deserves the hand they are dealt, good or bad."

Petula stopped what she was doing and unconsciously hugged the shirt she'd been inspecting close to her chest. This is exactly the kind of generic feel-good pabulum that would have sent her into a rage a few months earlier.

Scarlet saw Petula's eyes water and lips begin to tremble and realized that her sister's hobby had a lot less to do with her own situation or the unlucky in this world, than it did with what happened in the other one.

"Virginia wasn't your fault," Scarlet began somberly.

Petula froze. Scarlet understood much more than she thought, possibly even more than she herself did.

"And all the tricked-out homeless people in the world won't bring her back."

Chapter 19

Love the One You're With

You can't teach an old dogma new tricks.
–Dorothy Parker

You always hurt
the one you love.

When someone wants to go on a "break" from a relationship, but they assure you that you are the one for them, you can be sure that they're lying. They are pretty much saying, I don't want you around right now because I'm afraid someone better might come along and I'll miss that person because I'll be with you. The bottom line is, when you truly love someone, a "break" would only break your heart.

t was a Friday night and IdentiTea was jam-packed, as usual, with rockers, dark-wavers, and hipsters. But tonight the "it" crowd included the coolest kids on both spiritual planes, which made it the place to be for everyone who *is* or *was* anyone to be. It was the perfect setting for the kind of accidental meeting Charlotte had planned.

Damen had just arrived and scanned the room for Scarlet as he made for the DJ booth, doing his best to avoid eye contact. She saw him come in and did the same.

"Remember," Charlotte advised. "Stick to the plan."

Charlotte felt like a ringmaster, trying to coax a bunch of unpredictable animals through her invisible hoops. She knew that it could go so very wrong very fast and that ultimately, she would need to count on The Wendys' and Darcy's brazenness and Scarlet's stubborn snarkiness to seal the deal.

Scarlet scurried around trying to find one of her aprons to wear over a killer vintage baby-doll dress. She may have been feeling nervous on the inside, but she appeared cool and collected as usual. Her bangs were straight, but the rest of her hair was teased a little. She looked like she should be walking a couture catwalk in Paris, not serving Darjeeling tea in Hawthorne.

Scarlet was also wearing her bright red matte lipstick again, which took Damen, who was setting up his gear, by surprise. It looked to him like a flirty signal to the world at large that she was back to her old self—and available.

Darcy and The Wendys arrived and stopped at the counter to make sure Scarlet saw them. Scarlet just glared at them and fastened her apron. Pam and Prue gave Charlotte the okay sign and waited outside.

"How's business?" Darcy asked snidely, looking over Scarlet's outfit.

"Never better," Scarlet snapped.

"Good thing you have so much more free time to spend working," Wendy Anderson cracked spitefully. "Being single and all."

The girls sauntered off to their front-row table, which was already set up with their favorite frozen light latte energy drinks and offered perfect sightlines to the DJ booth. They wanted to make sure that he saw them. Before long, it had gotten so crowded the girls could barely see each other, let alone Damen, so they took matters into their own hands.

The Wendys shoved people aside like celebrity bodyguards, blazing a trail that lead directly to Damen, whom Darcy

wiggled and jiggled her way toward. She hopped over the rope dividing him from the rest of the room and began to dance, gyrating slowly and waving her arms over her head, snapping her fingers in time like some desperate fan.

Damen saw her—it was impossible not to—but chose to ignore her. Charlotte was satisfied that things were going off without a hitch, but became very uncomfortable with the events that she had set in motion when she got a good look at Darcy's booty shaking and Scarlet's horrified face.

As Damen picked up the beat, so did Darcy, getting a little smile out of him for no other reason than her sheer determination. The crowd appreciated it too, and chants of "Go, Darcy" went up, encouraging her further and pissing Scarlet off even more.

"One Kensington down," Wendy Anderson whispered, "one to go."

A cup and saucer that had been moving closer and closer to the edge of Damen's stand was finally knocked to the floor by Darcy's swiveling hips.

The Wendys signaled imperiously to Scarlet to deal with the spill.

"Waitress," Wendy Thomas ordered, "clean up this mess."

Things were definitely a mess, Scarlet thought as she walked over, and this wasn't the only one that needed cleaning.

"You mean your life or the teacup?" Scarlet shot back, as she bent down to pick up the shards.

It was so loud, between the crowd and the music, that Damen barely noticed what was going down between Scarlet and The Wendys. When Scarlet popped up from the floor, he

was shocked to find himself face-to-face with her. Neither of them knew what to say.

"Any requests?" was the best he could do, hoping maybe they could communicate as they always had, through music.

"I have one," Darcy said to Damen, cutting in before Scarlet could manage a word. "Will you go the prom with me?"

Scarlet laughed, knowing damn well that Damen would never go to the prom with Darcy, no matter how she treated him.

"Why not," Damen accepted. "The station is sending me to DJ there anyway."

Scarlet was shocked and flashed him a scathing look.

Darcy began her victory lap, eventually returning to her table with The Wendys, who couldn't be happier about the public dissing they'd just given Scarlet. In some ways, it was even more satisfying for them than Petula's trial.

"Nice one," Scarlet huffed, showing her disgust at Damen's cooperation with her most hated enemies.

"Nice lipstick," Damen shot back sarcastically, wanting Scarlet to know he got the message.

"It's really me, don't you think?" Scarlet said defiantly as she turned her back on him and walked away.

"I guess it really is," Damen whispered.

Charlotte paced the alley behind IdentiTea, waiting for Scarlet to leave. She longed to reach out to her.

"Waiting for someone?" Eric asked, startling her.

"I was just going to talk to Scarlet," she said. "But now that you're here, I guess I'll get going."

"Charlotte, you don't have to do this," he said.

"Do what?" she asked.

"If you want to see her, I'll leave," he said. "I know she said she had something to tell you."

Charlotte feared that that "something" was probably along the lines of "leave me alone and get out of my life," which is something she could not bear.

"I just want to know that she's okay, after everything with Damen," Charlotte said. "Especially after tonight."

Eric could only imagine what had gone on. He felt badly for Charlotte and only wanted to help, but whatever he said seemed to come out wrong.

"I'll check on her," he volunteered.

"Great," Charlotte said with an edge to her voice. "At least she won't be alone."

ॐ

Scarlet nursed a chai latte and a bruised ego for the rest of the evening, counting the seconds until closing time. The Wendys and Darcy split early, their self-satisfied grins on display, and in an effort to avoid another confrontation, Damen slinked out the back door. As the crowd emptied and the last straggler departed, Eric came in.

"How are you?" he asked.

"I just forced my boyfriend to go to the prom with another girl," Scarlet answered, tersely. "Apart from that, I'm fine."

"Ex-boyfriend," Eric said, reminding Scarlet of her comment from the day before.

"Right," Scarlet corrected herself wanly. "Ex-boyfriend."

Eric sensed an opportunity. Not just to comfort Scarlet, but

to help her channel some of the emotions she was feeling into something constructive, something that might benefit both of them.

"I always find that I'm at my best," Eric said leadingly, "when I'm at my worst."

Scarlet wasn't sure where he was going but the need not only to vent, but to really work out how she was feeling, was overwhelming.

He put both hands out, as if he were escorting her to the guitar sitting on the stand.

"Let's do it," she said.

❧

Charlotte was too agitated to head back to Damen's and after a long while found herself wandering toward the Kensington house, hoping that Scarlet would be home soon and that maybe Eric would not be with her. It was time to come clean about everything, she thought. When she arrived, she noticed a light on in an upstairs bedroom, which alarmed her. What if they're together, Charlotte thought, hanging out, laughing, listening to music, or worse. But it was Petula, not Scarlet, who was burning the midnight oil.

Charlotte walked in through the front door, as she had before, and up the stairs. It was a memory almost as vivid as arriving at Hawthorne Manor for the first time. She poked her head through Petula's door and, surprisingly, into an empty room. No Petula, but it was just as well. If ever there was a place, Charlotte thought, to get some insight about guys and relationships, it was here, among Petula's collection of diaries,

scrapbooks, photo albums, keepsakes, and love letters. It was a veritable archive of unrequited love, a catalog of rejection that she maintained to keep score of everyone who had tried and failed to win her.

As Charlotte flipped through the three-ring binder of mash notes, all of which Petula had graded from A through F, she was startled to see the bedroom door push open and Petula walk in. At least she thought it was Petula, hidden behind a load of clothes she was carrying from another room.

It wasn't just the obstructed view that made Petula hard for Charlotte to see. The girl she saw in front of her was someone she barely recognized. And the girl Charlotte had known and idolized, the girl who had lived in a life-size mirror, was gone. Dead.

As Charlotte stood staring at her, Petula felt a chill, as if she were being watched.

"Virginia?" Petula called out, hopefully, almost longingly.

Where Charlotte had once thought nothing of invading Petula's privacy, even her body, for a little taste of her glamazing life, it was almost too much for her to be part of such an intimate moment now. Petula looked like a child waiting for a reward that would never come.

Charlotte sought out Petula looking for advice about trivial things but was reminded instead about what was really important.

Chapter
20

All Tomorrow's Parties

Loneliness is a crowded room

–Bryan Ferry

Friend or foe.

The great thing about having an enemy is that you know exactly where that person stands. You can't be surprised by a backstab because you know always to be on your guard. In fact, their opposition to you actually helps to make you sharper, by forcing you to justify your own actions and opinions, sometimes even to yourself. If you want sympathy, look for a friend, but if you want honesty, an enemy might be the best friend you ever had.

carlet and Eric were still at IdentiTea, alone in the dark except for a single candle burning between them.

"Was that good for you?" Eric asked.

"Amazing," Scarlet said, trying to catch her breath.

"We should do it again."

"I don't think I can," Scarlet confessed wearily.

"Okay," Eric went on, "As long as you're satisfied."

"I definitely am."

"Then let's hear the playback," Eric suggested.

"Let's," she agreed nervously.

She pushed aside her mic, jumped up, and headed over to the café mixing board she used to record live performances onstage. She pressed the Back button, then Play, and they both listened to every measure carefully as the track flowed through the speakers.

"Now that," Eric paused for effect, "is *rock*."

"Really?" Scarlet said incredulously. "I don't know."

"You put your heart into it," Eric said admiringly. "Every word."

"And you put your soul into every note."

Eric just smiled. She didn't know how right she was.

As if on cue, Charlotte came to the front door and looked in. Scarlet saw her and quietly freaked that she was caught in what may have appeared to be a compromising position. Charlotte got flustered at seeing Scarlet and Eric and ran. And when Scarlet turned back to Eric, he too looked like he'd just seen a ghost. But he couldn't have, she thought, could he?

"What's wrong?" Scarlet asked, her curiosity suddenly turning to suspicion.

"Nothing," Eric mumbled sheepishly.

"Did you see that person in the doorway?"

"What girl?"

"I didn't say it was a girl, Eric," Scarlet said.

He was busted. Scarlet began to rewind their entire relationship in her head and came to the only obvious conclusion.

"Do you have something you want to tell me?" Scarlet asked.

"What are you talking about?" Eric asked.

Scarlet paused, giving Eric time to step up and be honest with her.

"You're dead."

From the look on her face, Eric couldn't tell if she meant she was going to kill him or if she had figured out the whole thing. Still, part of him was relieved and thought it was time he rocked the truth.

"Why didn't you tell me?" she asked, her tone becoming angrier by the second.

Eric was silent. Scarlet didn't push it. The real culprit here was Charlotte anyway. How could Charlotte keep this from her? And then it occurred to Scarlet.

"The girl you wrote the song for," Scarlet said. "It was Charlotte."

Everything was starting to make sense.

"I wanted to tell you," he said.

"Why didn't you?" she asked.

"It just never came up," Eric said, grasping at straws. "Anyway, I had no idea you'd be able to see me."

"Yeah, it's a real gift," Scarlet said sarcastically. "What are you doing here anyway?"

"I don't really know," Eric said, "but I'm gonna guess that it has something to do with helping you work some things out for yourself. And judging from what we did here tonight, I think I've done my job."

"I appreciate the song," Scarlet said, "I really do, but this Angels Anonymous crap has done nothing but screw things up for me."

"You're not the only one," Eric said. "We're all paying a price for being here."

Scarlet tried not to sympathize, but she couldn't help it. She could see on his pale face the sacrifice he was making.

"Do me a favor," Scarlet asked. "Don't tell Charlotte I know."

"We're not really talking," Eric said, "so that won't be too difficult."

"Because of me?" Scarlet asked, guilt-ridden.

Eric just nodded. Knowing Eric, even the short time she had spent with him, she knew how Charlotte must have fallen for him and how threatened she must have felt by Scarlet's relationship with him. She must have felt like he was emotionally cheating on her which, in Scarlet's mind and certainly in Charlotte's, was even worse than physically cheating.

"So Darcy and Damen," Scarlet continued in junior detective mode, "is to make me see the error of my ways?"

"Among other things," Eric said, nodding.

"If Charlotte weren't dead, I would kill her."

"She's feeling really bad about it already," Eric said. "That's probably why she came back just now. To tell you."

"Damen's letter," Scarlet said, mostly talking to herself. "I know she was there when he wrote it. She helped him to write those things I needed him to say."

Eric just smiled, impressed that Scarlet put it all together.

As her anger subsided, an odd feeling swept over Scarlet. She had been singing, laughing, talking, and fighting with a dead guy.

"What happened to you?" Scarlet asked.

"I was onstage getting ready to play my first real show," he began to recount painfully. "It was about to storm, but everyone thought it would pass quickly."

"But the only thing that passed...," she said somberly.

"Was me," Eric concluded. "I got electrocuted when lightning hit my amp."

"Sorry," she offered.

"It's okay, I'm over it," he said, but the look on his face told her quite the opposite.

"So you never got to play in front of a crowd?"

"Nope."

"Let's see what we can do about that," Scarlet said, grabbing the flash drive with their new song from the board and putting it in her pocket.

❦

Darcy and The Wendys zipped through town after spending the whole day filling up on ridiculously expensive makeup, soaps, perfume, and undergarments, not to mention inane conversation, all in the name of prom.

"Who do you think Petula is going with?" Wendy Anderson asked, unsure if she should care or not.

"Why do you care?" Darcy snapped from the driver's seat of Wendy's convertible.

"Oh, right, I don't," Wendy Anderson said from the passenger seat. "I just forgot for a sec."

Wendy Thomas took the opportunity to cackle hysterically at her fellow Wendy's self-esteem smackdown.

"Push your seat up," Wendy Thomas said, kicking the back and causing Wendy to jerk forward. "I'm going to get a blood clot back here."

"Next time, you sit up front then," Wendy Anderson complained. "It's not my fault you were born with freakishly long tibias…no offense."

"Just because you say no offense doesn't make it okay, Wendy."

Darcy ignored The Wendys' chatter and slowed down to scope out the side streets.

"Check it out," Darcy said, pointing.

It was Petula, leaning up against the side of her car talking to someone. She was handing over suit jackets and slacks to a young man.

Darcy beeped the horn.

"Quick, give me that bag," she said to Wendy Anderson.

Wendy threw her the bag and Darcy grabbed some soaps. She rolled down her window and chucked them out at Petula and the derelict.

"Hey, that's mine!" Wendy Thomas scowled. "Those were totally natural, cold-process, Soil Association–Certified soaps you just tossed!"

"Write it off as a charitable donation," Darcy spat, tossing her tax lawyer's business card into the backseat.

Wendy didn't know much about giving, but she knew enough to keep a receipt. She checked her purse and breathed a sigh a relief when she found it, folded neatly.

As the Hawthorne harpies sped off, Petula opened the bag and saw the luxury cleansing bars as well as Tate's raised eyebrows.

"Oh, those were my friends," Petula said, eyeing the product. "I asked them to pick some of this up for me. High-end stuff."

"You don't have to cover for them," Tate said.

"You're right, I don't," she said. "They threw a bar of soap at us because you're dirty…and they aren't my friends. Anymore."

She was so relieved to tell the truth. She was relieved to be herself and to go after what she wanted, despite what others

thought. It was liberating. CoCo would have been proud. She led her to him, but Petula was the one who did all the hard work.

"Would you go to my prom with me?" she asked.

He didn't answer her but instead gave her a peck on the cheek.

She was disappointed, but she knew he cared for her.

"You never answered my question the other day," he said. "What are you doing here?"

"These people may be starving or whatever," Petula said, not quite expert in the linguistic subtleties of the downtrodden, "but they can still look their best."

His first reaction was that she was hopelessly naive to the point of ignorance. But then it dawned on him that Petula understood something that even most well-intentioned politicians, pundits, and philanthropists didn't: self-esteem is the best medicine for malaise. And she was helping them the way she knew how. The proof was right in front of him. Petula made each of them over and brought some beauty into their lives.

Tate took the soap out of her hands.

"Looks like I might be needing this," he said.

"You're going to go with me?"

After watching her put smiles on face after face, night after night, Tate tenderly accepted Petula's offer and put a smile on hers, as well.

֎

Stylus barged into the studio just as Damen was about to end his shift. He'd been assigned the long and tedious job of digitizing tracks from all the vinyl albums they had in the

studio archive. He was bleary-eyed and smelled like a mildewy mixture of plastic and damp cardboard. Even Charlotte, who didn't need sleep, was exhausted just from watching him.

"Dylan," Mr. Stylus grumbled, tossing over a CD like a Frisbee. "Catch."

Damen's athleticism served him well as he plucked the disc from the air and flipped it over to read the credit. The name on the disc, written in Magic Marker, read: "'Kiss Your Kiss'/ Scarlet Kensington."

"I thought you said she was disqualified," Damen said, surprised not just by the addition of the song but that it even existed.

"It's new," Stylus explained in his morning-shift baritone. "Just came in under the wire. It's your girlfriend's, right?"

"Ex-girlfriend," Damen clarified, thinking to himself how little time remained in the competition.

"Bad for you, good for the song," the station manager gruffed. "As long as you're not on it, it's allowed. Load it in."

Damen had mixed feelings as he watched the control room computer rip the song off the CD and convert it into a music file. She did it without him, and he couldn't bear that. He left the studio as the song was loading.

❧

"IdentiTea," Scarlet answered trepidatiously, and a little hopefully, after noticing that the caller ID on the café phone displayed the number from the radio station.

"Is this Scarlet Kensington?" the caller asked in a big, echoey voice.

"Yeah, who wants to know?" she replied in her token jaded tone after it was clear that it wasn't Damen.

"Mr. Stylus, INDY-Ninety-five Morning Man," the station manager advised. "You're on the air."

"So," she replied, thinking maybe this was some kind of prank or worse, a love-line intervention.

"We were wondering if you've picked a location," he said.

"You're sitting on it."

"That's a good one," he said in a cheesy radio-announcer voice, "but I don't think you could fit a guitar in there, although with this new fiber diet I'm trying, maybe!"

Scarlet's instincts were right, she thought. He was an ass.

"What's this about?" she asked, trying to keep her composure.

"We want to know where and when you'll be playing your song live," he said. "You can pick any venue in town."

"What?" she asked, her mood brightening in anticipation.

"That's the prize for…THE WINNING SONG."

Stylus rolled the goofy marching band tape and hit the fireworks sound effects that signaled her victory to all of his listeners. Instead of being cheesed out, Scarlet was blushing with pride.

"Are you messing with me?" she asked, her cheeks now hot and in full, rosy bloom.

"What's going on?" Eric asked, wondering if some degenerate had called in to harass her.

"We won," she mouthed, not wanting to disturb the paying customers. "We get to pick a place around town to play our song."

"We're gonna play in front of people?" he asked in shock.

It was definitely a life-and-death dream come true for him; but for her, it was the perfect opportunity.

"Well, where would you like to play, and when?" the announcer asked.

"I have just the place," Scarlet said.

☙

"You win," Marianne said, throwing up her hands at the prom committee meeting. "What do you want us to do?"

"This is something I've been thinking about a long time," she began.

Scarlet explained her idea and instructed them on what was to be done. She insisted it all be shrouded in secrecy because if a certain trio, Damen, or Charlotte found out about it, her plans could be ruined. With everyone on board and so little time to pull everything off, preparations got under way immediately.

Aside from being obsessed with all the details of the night, Scarlet was working diligently to find the perfect dress for the occasion. And although Damen was nowhere to be found, he too was at the forefront of her mind. Still, it was necessary to keep him in the dark, because that meant keeping Charlotte clueless as well.

Scarlet wasn't the only one with a plan for prom, however. Pam, Prue, and Charlotte were busy planning something a little more sinister: Darcy's demise. They decided that the prom was the best place to do it since everyone would be distracted, and hopefully, if things went off without a hitch, the

real Darcy could reinhabit her body without anyone being the wiser.

Charlotte knew they had little control over the outcome, so she left it up to fate. She was sure that Scarlet would probably never talk to her again, and she didn't blame her one bit, but she did want her to be happy. If that meant sacrificing her friendship, something she cherished more than anything, then she would do that.

"What are we going to do exactly?" Pam asked.

"Kill her," Prue said matter-of-factly. "That's what."

"I don't think I can kill anyone," Pam said, "especially on prom night."

৩৩

Petula was hurriedly palming through frock after frock, this time for herself, at Dressed to Kill. It was her last stop of the day, following a pretty fruitless search for a prom dress. Ordinarily she would have had her pick of the litter for such a special occasion, but things were different now.

Petula was surprisingly serene about it, now that her priorities had changed. After rummaging through rack after rack and finding nothing, she looked up at the cash register to see a beautiful red sequined gown bagged and hanging. Petula eyed it covetously. As the fashion bell went off in her head, the doorbell went off in the shop, which Petula saw initially as a good sign.

She approached the salesperson, flashing her plastic, ready to snap it up.

"I'll take it," Petula said, still not used to having to explain herself.

"What do you mean?" the clerk asked, "A job application?"

"The dress." Petula pointed. "It was absolutely made for me."

"No," a voice came sternly from behind her, "it was made for *me*."

Petula spun around and came face-to-face with Darcy, then slid her credit card back into her wallet.

"Isn't your ass a little big for that gown?" Petula cut. "Prom will be over by the time you get into it."

"I'm sure Damen only cares how fast it comes off," Darcy cracked. "I'll get back to you on that."

Darcy snuck in a twofer. Not only did she just retro-dis Petula's and Damen's relationship but she dissed Scarlet as well.

"I love what you've done with your hair," the salesclerk said, trying to protect her customer.

"Home perm?" Petula snapped.

Darcy was thrown for a second by the hair cuts and reflexively checked herself in the store mirror. She noticed the salesclerk chuckling along with Petula and re-engaged in the bitchy banter.

"What are you doing here anyway?" Darcy asked, picking away. "You don't buy clothes anymore; you donate them."

"I don't just give things away," Petula insisted, turning back to Darcy. "I'm a social entrepreneur."

"More like a social leper, I'd say," Darcy pushed back. "Hey, maybe prom can double as a friend-raiser for you? Everyone is into helping those less fortunate these days, ain't that right?"

Petula walked back menacingly toward Darcy, who held her ground.

"I have real friends now," Petula said. "Besides, you didn't take anything away from me. I let you have it."

"I never look a gift horse-face in the mouth," Darcy swiped, feigning a whinny. "I'm happy to take it all."

"Now who's the charity case?" Petula snipped.

"You can always just stop," Darcy suggested casually, looking through the rack in front of her and keeping one eye on Petula. "I'm sure I could persuade The Wendys to let you hit the Reset button."

Petula's future flashed before her eyes — the future she had planned and plotted for herself before now. She could see it all, except for herself. She was no longer there.

"People change," Petula said simply. "I don't need the echo chamber anymore."

"You are an egomaniac with a guilt complex, that's all," Darcy remarked, drilling down deep in search of Petula's motivation. "This is about you, not about helping those losers downtown."

"Psychobabble from a psychobitch," Petula said calmly. "How enlightening."

"You are not making one bit of difference," Darcy pressed, seeming a tad frustrated. "And you're trashing perfectly good outfits in the process."

"You seem to know a lot about trash," Petula smiled sweetly.

"Not as much as your prom date, I hear," Darcy said, grinning widely, then turned back to the salesclerk, who was halfway hiding beneath the counter, hoping to avoid the fallout from any exchange between them. "I'll have the dress now."

Petula watched helplessly as Darcy handed over her charge card and signed the charge receipt.

"I think they have one left in beige in a bigger size that you might want to consider," Darcy suggested, heading out the door.

"You can try to look like me, dress like me, even lure my flunkies away," Petula squawked. "But there was only one me."

"True," Darcy preened. "I am the *new* you."

Petula stared at Darcy as she passed by her, not so much in anger as in recognition of what she herself had been and what she could easily become again.

"Hey, Petula, I'm looking for some part-time work," Darcy inquired snidely. "Are there any unclaimed Dumpsters you can recommend?"

"No," Petula answered, "but I know some girls downtown who are hiring. You're a natural."

"As long as I look good," Darcy said, fingering her trophy gown, "it doesn't matter what I do."

"Or who," Petula interjected for spite.

"Later, Coma Toes." Darcy began to giggle disrespectfully, swinging her dress back and forth like a carrot on a stick. "I'll be you later."

☙❧

Petula walked into her bedroom. It was dark, but she didn't bother to flip the light switch. She was alone and dressless. This was prom and she had nothing to wear. Losing her status at school was one thing, but losing it at retail was an entirely different matter.

She made her way over to her bed in tears and tried to come up with a creative idea. She was good at dressing others lately, but now, when it came to herself, she had nothing left. She rolled over and buried her head in her pillow and, as she did, she felt something. It wasn't her comforter; it was much more substantial than that. It was heavy, and she could feel its beauty before she even flicked on the light.

"Holy Dolce and Gabbana," she gasped, as close to a religious exclamation as she could muster, wiping the tears from her eyes.

There it was, lying next to her, a soft pink chiffon vintage Chanel dress. It was gorgeous, archive-worthy, something to be worshipped at a gala thrown in its honor, or even better, studied behind glass. In other words, perfect for her.

Petula delicately stepped into the dress, savoring every detail of the material. It was the sugarless icing on her carob cake. And, it wasn't just the gown that was perfect, the fit was too. She slinked up to the mirror and checked herself out, scrupulously. *The Wendys and Darcy had better prepare*, Petula thought to herself. She was dressed for battle now.

"There is a God," Petula sighed, certain she would be wearing the most beautiful dress at the prom.

"I thought you'd like it," Scarlet said casually, walking by Petula's door without so much glancing in.

She wasn't exactly Petula's God, but Scarlet was just the unlikely style-savvy savior she needed.

Chapter
21

Charlotte Sometimes

Whatever this world can give me,
It's you, you're all I see.
—Queen

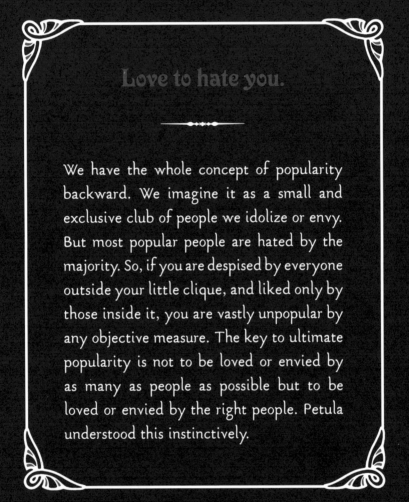

Love to hate you.

We have the whole concept of popularity backward. We imagine it as a small and exclusive club of people we idolize or envy. But most popular people are hated by the majority. So, if you are despised by everyone outside your little clique, and liked only by those inside it, you are vastly unpopular by any objective measure. The key to ultimate popularity is not to be loved or envied by as many as people as possible but to be loved or envied by the right people. Petula understood this instinctively.

The night couldn't have been more perfect as everyone descended on Hawthorne High, dressed to impress. Gossip was flying about who showed up with whom, who was wearing what, and who the best- and worst-dressed were. The comments were brutal enough to make a Tinseltown blogger blush. It was a night where everyone would say goodbye, to each other and to the confines of high school. Freedom was so close they could taste it.

Damen was set up and spinning at the DJ booth, rattling the bleachers as his beats pumped throughout the room and the seniors started arriving. The Wendys made a typically over-the-top entrance in a twenty-foot-long Ferrari Modena limo, complete with gull-wing doors. They didn't so much exit the car as they were revealed when the doors retracted upward.

As they stepped out in the most stunning outfits, the pair made sure their dates were three paces behind and safely out of the frames before posing for pictures. The Wendys planted themselves in poses and then moved their heads from right to left with abrupt precision, stopping and pausing at exact intervals like automatic sprinkler heads as they posed for each photographer and literally put their best faces forward. Wendy

Anderson rocked a white ball gown with a fitted, beaded bodice, and Wendy Thomas wore a super-sexy, backless green floor-length number from an exclusive boutique in town.

They'd been absolutely promonstrous in their quest, bullying just about every dress shop owner and local designer they could find into holding one-of-a-kind pieces for them to try. They all cooperated, however resentfully, realizing that, with Petula completely out of favor, having The Wendys wear one of their dresses would provide just the sales bump they needed.

Their dates were secondary to the dresses, just additional accessories. Wendy Anderson was escorted by the captain of the football team, of course, and Wendy Thomas was there with Gorey High's QB, Josh Valence. Josh was the guy who had dumped Petula like a dirty rag and left her comatose — literally. It was actually Darcy's idea for Wendy Thomas to bring him, even though she admitted to not knowing him very well. It was just another way to add insult to Petula's injury.

"What is this?" Wendy Anderson asked as they walked into the lobby of the school and saw the huge banner draped across the gym entrance.

"Where is the Night of Our Lives banner?" Wendy Anderson bristled.

"It was changed," Marianne said indifferently, taking their tickets.

"By whom?" Wendy Thomas asked, pushing her date aside. "Night of Our Lives is the perfect theme!"

"We demand to see your supervisor!" Wendy Anderson added, trying to help.

"I heard that some girl got to pick the theme at the last

minute," Marianne said, not wanting to let on that she knew anything about it. "She won a radio contest or something."

Wendy Anderson had a sinking suspicion as to what girl she was talking about, and it was only a matter of seconds before Wendy Thomas caught on. They couldn't be certain because they only listened to pop stations.

"Nobody gets to screw with our memories," Wendy Anderson cautioned.

"But you're not the only ones here," Marianne responded rationally, "making memories."

"We *are* their memories!" Wendy Thomas said, pointing her acrylic-tipped index finger imperiously at the masses.

☙❧

Charlotte, Prue, and Pam arrived in the lobby just as The Wendys were causing a ruckus. Prue and Pam chalked up the super-bratty behavior to their all-juice pre-prom cleanses and proceeded to ignore them, preferring to take in the excitement of the event instead.

Charlotte, meanwhile, was lost in thought and couldn't help feeling sad. She'd longed for prom since she was small. Never in her wildest dreams could she have imagined not living to see it. Now, here it was, right in front of her eyes, and she was…alone.

Prom was the first stop on the road to adulthood, one that had turned into a dead end. She was okay with all of that, but she wasn't okay with the fact that Eric was going with her best friend. It all seemed so wrong.

Charlotte didn't have much time to stew in her feelings,

however, as Darcy came through the door, fashionably late of course. Darcy, in a skintight, red sequined, strapless gown, flaunting her kill-them-with-envy body, slithered down the waxed hall and straight for The Wendys. They'd decided to enter the room together dramatically, officially debuting their new power trio to what they fully expected would be wild enthusiasm from the assembly.

Unfortunately, it was not to be.

"Change of plans," Darcy advised, smoothing the small wrinkles from her hips. "I'm going to the DJ booth."

"Do you want us to back you?" Wendy Anderson asked, trying to hang on to a little limelight. "It might get rough with Scarlet or even Petula in there."

"You guys can keep my seat at the table," Darcy snipped, leaving no question who the star of this show was. "I want to walk in alone."

The Wendys nodded discontentedly. Even Petula at her worst wouldn't have treated them so shabbily in public, they thought.

"I'm going to get this guy," Darcy said to herself, fussing with the cutlets in her strapless bra, "if it's the last thing I do."

"It will be," Charlotte promised. "I guarantee it."

☙☙

Charlotte, Pam, and Prue knew they had a big job ahead of them, but as they approached the doors to the gym they stopped, stood together, and allowed themselves a moment. This would be the only prom that any of them would ever attend. It was every girl's dream, theirs included, and one they each had believed would remain unfulfilled.

Whatever the ups and downs of being back, whatever they were required to do for others, this was a gift for them, as well. They might not have the pretty corsages or expensive dresses that other girls demanded, but they did have the greatest prom dates anyone could ask for: they had each other.

"Are we ready?" Pam asked, gripping Charlotte's hand.

"It's showtime," Prue said, starting toward the entryway.

Charlotte pulled away for a second, her nerves getting the best of her. It felt almost like when they crossed over from Fall Ball, except the opposite. Both moments were filled with anticipation, but she preferred the unknown scenario to this one, which she could imagine far too easily—and painfully.

"You guys go first," Charlotte said.

"See you in there, okay?" Pam said, smiling softly.

"Don't punk out on us," Prue warned. "We're counting on you."

"Eric's the punk, not me, remember?" Charlotte smiled a kind of pre-vomit grin at them. "I'll be right in."

Charlotte prepared herself as Pam and Prue walked in ahead. It wasn't the prom fantasy she had in mind, seeing her boyfriend there with her best friend, but if everything worked out between Damen and Scarlet and if Darcy was stopped, then it would all be worth it.

She couldn't help wondering if this was what Markov had really had in mind when he sent them back. It was all about the little things, he said, but all this drama was playing out on the widescreen in her mind.

As Pam and Prue entered they were surprised to find The Wendys still standing stock-still just inside the doorway,

looking all around the room with some mixture of astonishment and disgust. A quick glance up and they understood why. The smiles on their faces, they were sure, would be no match for Charlotte's when she finally came in. She could never have been prepared for what she was about to see.

In the lobby, Charlotte visualized her moves like an Olympic gymnast about to take the vault before she finally talked herself into entering the gym. She closed her eyes, tightened up, and walked stiffly toward the doors, hoping Pam and Prue would be on the other side to "spot" her.

She stood silently, as Pam and Prue beamed at her, unable to find words to describe the sight of an entire room completely encased in the most lush, gorgeous flowers — red roses and deep purple calla lilies as far as the eye could see. They crept up the walls and dripped, as if they were weeping from the tented ceiling and the temporarily installed candlelight chandeliers. Enormous floor-to-ceiling sculptures of mournful, statuesque angels looked over the room, their wings folded to protect and their heads tilted in sympathy. The room was transformed into some magical Architectural Digest version of a designer graveyard and fantastical funeral parlor.

"What's going on?" Charlotte asked, finally uttering a few coherent syllables.

"Surprise," Prue said under her breath, still barely able to speak herself.

"It looks like a fantasy funeral to me," Pam said, pointing to the fresh flower banner overhead.

Hanging above her was a living collage that spelled out "Charlotte 'ghostgirl' Usher" in thousands of red roses, com-

plete with dates of birth and death. It was profoundly touching and unbelievably surreal and even a little weird to see people grinding away on the dance floor and having such a good time at her memorial. But she wouldn't have it any other way.

"Killer prom," one group of stag guys shouted, high-fiving themselves in a vain effort to get the attention of a group of single hotties dancing next to them.

"A surprise fantasy funeral?" Charlotte mouthed out loud. "For me?"

"I think this is probably the first and only surprise funeral," Pam said, affectionately making Charlotte feel even more special.

"Somebody down here likes you," Prue said.

Charlotte touched her chest and felt for something that wasn't there, but that she could all of a sudden feel. What Scarlet had created for her was indescribable. It was gorgeous and classy, like a fairy tale. Or a state funeral fit for a beloved princess, but it was also prom, the most important night of a teen's life, which only added to the sentiment. Best of all, Charlotte noted, everything was Charlotte-themed with her favorite songs, colors, and flowers.

Many in the crowd had worn black, in keeping with the theme, and Damen blackened the mood, in a good way, cross-fading into "Funeral Party" by The Cure as everyone floated around the room, elegantly celebrating Charlotte's life and death. They all looked like beautiful, choreographed marionettes waltzing to a mournful symphony.

Not everyone was enjoying the scene, however.

"A funeral-themed prom?" Wendy Anderson spouted, banging her fist. "I swear I could just kill someone."

"Are you taking suggestions?" Prue added.

Chapter
22

Femme Fatale

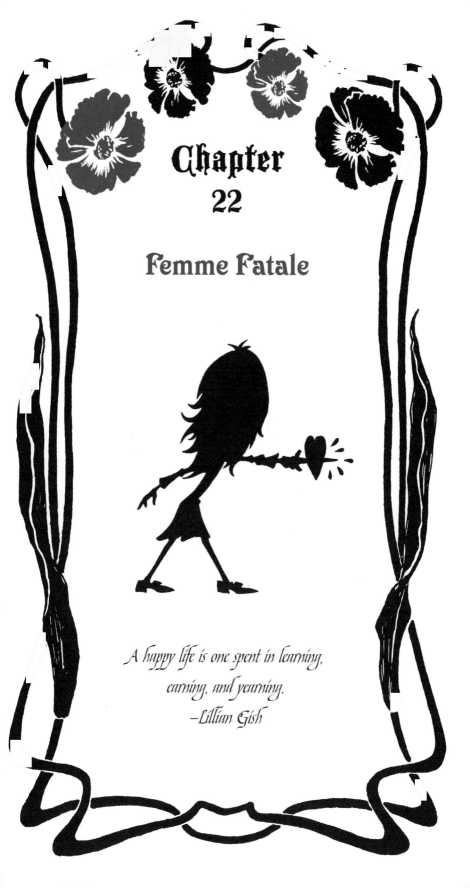

A happy life is one spent in learning,
earning, and yearning.
—Lillian Gish

Off-limits.

We like to think there are some things we would never do. Standards that we set to guide us through even the most difficult circumstances. Depending on what's at stake, however, we may find ourselves thinking and acting in ways we could never have imagined. It's easy to draw a line in the sand, but sometimes it's hard to find that line when the wind begins to blow.

laytime is over," Prue said, eyeing the line forming at the photo station. Charlotte was still nearly breathless as she passed by the gorgeously appointed tables, each one sporting an elaborate candelabra cremation urn, overflowing with flowers and with gold-plated toe tags hanging around the base as placeholders. The videographer was filming couples all prepping for their YouTube "eulogies," which would be posted on the school's website and then archived to be played again at future reunions.

"Everyone wants to be remembered," Charlotte sighed as she took her place behind Prue.

The threesome made their way over to the line where guests were waiting anxiously to get their pictures taken. Damen had promised to get his picture taken with Darcy, whom he figured wanted some kind of verifiable proof of the event, but he

was most anxious about running into Scarlet. He still wasn't sure if she was coming, but if she did, he heard it would be with some guy nobody knew or had seen before. Leave it to Scarlet to keep everyone guessing.

"This better work," Pam said, hoping the plan wouldn't backfire, like everything else had lately.

"You mean trying to get away with offing somebody in a roomful of people," Prue sneered. "Yeah, it better work."

Even though it was Charlotte's plan, she couldn't believe they were actually plotting a murder.

They'd thought of all the ways they could "do her in" and reviewed ways that teens had checked out in the past: trying to fit into a size two dress when you're a six, getting hit by a limo, subway surfing, falling off the stage at the grand march, and there was the classic anaphylactic shock from a corsage allergy. But none of them would work in Darcy's case. It was all pretty creepy actually, but Charlotte kept reminding herself it was a kind of self-defense, and, if all went well, would be reversible. At least she hoped so.

"Time to execute," Charlotte said, pun barely intended.

"Next!" the greasy ponytailed headbanger in the threadbare powder-blue tux said as he snapped each couple's picture. For them this was the most important part of the evening, the part they would carry in their wallets, frame for their parents, hide from their future wives or husbands in years to come, but to him it was routine business.

Charlotte looked around to see where everyone was, but there was no sign of Petula. Not seeing Petula at the prom was unsettling. Charlotte needed that comfort for what was about

to go down. For her, it was like having a celebrity on your flight. It made her feel as though the plane, or in this case, the plan, wouldn't go down in flames.

"Places, everybody!" Charlotte ordered, barking stage directions since she didn't really know gangster lingo.

The line moved quickly, and Damen and Darcy were next. Prue, Pam, and Charlotte took their positions—Pam behind Damen, Prue behind Darcy, and Charlotte behind the photographer.

"Hello," Darcy cooed, working the photographer so that they could get a few extra shots.

The photographer recited the standard rules and disclaimer as he did for each couple as Damen and Darcy positioned themselves to be memorialized.

"Your photo will be sent to you in an obituary format, so you're going to need to fill out the forms over there for the mock article on you both as a couple, and today you'll get a receipt that's a 'pray we make it' couple mass card with your picture on it. You will need that to claim your obit once they're in."

"Together forever," Darcy said.

Just then, Scarlet walked in, completely covered in a vintage long, blond faux fur coat, with Eric by her side, unseen of course by everyone but Pam, Prue, and Charlotte. She stopped to take in the surreal scene playing out in front of her, so intently focused on Damen that she didn't even react to Charlotte at the tripod.

Damen looked extremely uneasy and red-faced. The whole memorial theme was really getting to him. This was not the way he hoped to be remembered, posing like a cardboard

cutout next to a self-absorbed girl who meant nothing to him. If that was his life plan, he would have just stayed with Petula. He stared back at Scarlet blankly while Darcy flashed a victorious smirk.

"Don't get distracted," Eric nudged, trying to comfort Scarlet and keep her focused as he gently ushered her toward the gym.

Charlotte, meanwhile, looked as if she'd seen a ghost, which, of course, she had.

Scarlet entered, but Eric hung back, looking over at Charlotte.

"Don't get distracted," Prue repeated to Charlotte, who was distressed not just about Eric, but also over the pain she was clearly causing Scarlet. "First things first."

The photographer played with the focus and locked them in his viewfinder for what seemed like an eternity to the angelic assassins. Finally, the moment arrived.

"Push it good," Prue sang evilly as Darcy and Damen posed in front of the backdrop. "Push it *real* good."

"Okay, now, on the count of three…," he said.

As he counted, Prue, Pam, and Charlotte counted right along with him.

"Say cheese," Prue smirked, reassuringly offering a "we can do this" nod to her friends.

"One. Two. Three!"

On three, Pam pushed Damen off the platform so he wouldn't be suspected of anything criminal. Prue held Darcy right in the camera shot while Charlotte forced the photog's finger down on the shutter, creating an almost continuous flash. The light was blinding.

Suddenly, Darcy dropped to the floor, shaking uncontrollably, but Charlotte kept the photog's finger from lifting off the camera trigger, continuing the blinding onslaught so that no one could see what was happening.

A flurry of activity began in the room, students and adult chaperones rushing the photo station to see what was going on and how they could help. Memories of Petula collapsing in his car set off alarm bells in Josh's head, and he decided to ditch Wendy. He panicked and backed away from the scene slowly, fearful of being blamed for yet another Hawthorne High hottie biting it.

"She's down!" Pam yelled.

"Down…"—Charlotte paused in anticipation for the result she'd been expecting—"and out."

A figure emerged in the flashes and Charlotte released the button, along with a sulfurous stink that could have been from the burnt-out bulb or the sudden arrival. Either way, it gave new meaning to "party pooper."

"Maddy," Charlotte muttered.

They all knew she would likely be the one to show up, but seeing her again, right there in front of them, was a bit shocking, to say the least. There she was, standing over Darcy's body with a slap-worthy smirk on her face. She hadn't changed a bit. Her hair was frizzy and she was still sporting bohemian chic—a long, flowery, floor-length spaghetti-strap dress, bangles, and long, dangling earrings.

"The party can start now!" Maddy announced, but her arrogance was short-lived as she felt herself being pulled away. "What the…"

"I'll be seeing you," Charlotte said, throwing Maddy's words from their last meeting back in her face.

"So far, so good," Pam smiled as she and Prue grabbed Maddy tightly.

The three of them vanished an instant later.

"Get the defibrillator!" Damen shouted into the gathering crowd as he hovered above Darcy.

"What defibrillator?" Marianne, the ever-earnest student council president yelled back. "We used the funds for that for new tubas! The new fund-raiser isn't scheduled for another year!"

Without any other alternative, Damen began chest compressions. He didn't like Darcy, but he wasn't going to let her die either. Scarlet watched from the side as he tried to save her rival, pulling for him proudly, but also watching where exactly he put his hands. She couldn't help it.

"This is taking too long," Charlotte said desperately. "She's got to be brought back *now*."

"If she *is* going to die," Wendy Anderson whispered to Wendy Thomas, as they scoped out the decor, "she's in the right place for it."

Charlotte didn't know what to do, and almost reflexively called out her boyfriend's name.

"Eric," Charlotte screamed. "Please help!"

Immediately responding to Charlotte's plea, Eric placed his right hand, the one he strummed with, on Darcy's chest, and then through her rib cage into her heart.

A bright light, mistaken by the crowd for an errant camera flash, exploded and crackled over the scene, and Damen was

thrown back a little by a jolt he felt through his entire body. Judging from the sudden heaving of Darcy's chest, she felt it too.

"They don't call me Electric Eric for nothing," Eric said to Charlotte with pride.

"I always said you had great hands," Charlotte said gratefully.

Everyone's eyes were on Darcy as she came to. Well, everyone except The Wendys. They were totally annoyed that Darcy had drawn so much attention to herself and away from them. The prom photographer had turned news photographer all of the sudden, documenting Darcy's near-fatal collapse. With the flash popping again, The Wendys did a quick cost-benefit analysis and bent down to her side with faux sincerity, hoping to glom a little publicity from this washout of an evening.

"Where am I?" Darcy asked, still foggy.

"You are at the Hawthorne High prom," Wendy Anderson said, more gently than anyone had ever heard her speak in public.

"With *us*," Wendy Thomas stressed, her eyes peeled for local news crews, as she grabbed one of Darcy's arms, carefully lifting her to a sitting position for a good group shot.

"Who are *you*?" the girl asked.

The crowd gasped with surprise and both Wendys, mortified, let her go. Damen shoved them both out of the way and helped Darcy, whose head hit the floor from the drop, back up. He could tell there was suddenly something different about her.

"Are you okay?" Damen asked.

"Yeah, I just don't remember much," Darcy said, completely coming to and unable to see any of the dead.

"It was so strange," she said. "I was just talking to some people, and now they're gone?"

"It is," Damen said, looking around for someone he knew he couldn't see, "very strange."

"I love that song," Darcy said out of nowhere.

"Thanks; it's from my mix tape," Damen said, realizing Darcy was maybe a little more like Scarlet than he'd thought at first. "You should stick around. It gets better."

"I'm not really much of a prom person," Darcy admitted, "but thanks."

Damen just smiled at Darcy and realized his instincts were right. She and Scarlet might even be friends under different circumstances. Probably best that she left anyway though. It seemed like she had a lot of questions that needed answering.

He waited a few minutes longer for the EMT to arrive, helped her into the ambulance, and headed back to the DJ booth as the crowd dispersed.

"I have to go," Eric said to Charlotte. "There's something I have to do."

Reality hit Charlotte like a ton of bricks. He was there with Scarlet, not her.

"Yeah, I have something I have to do too," she said glumly.

☙❧

As Charlotte arrived at the intake office, a ghostly intervention was already well under way.

"Let go of me," Maddy, pinned to the floor by Mary, Beth, and Sally, hissed. "Where am I?"

"It's not so important where you are," Prue spit, cryptically, "as where you're going."

"You can't keep me here," Maddy insisted, continuing to struggle.

"Yes, we can," Pam said. "You don't have a choice."

Charlotte walked in and straight to Maddy, getting in her face.

"Darcy died in school just now," Charlotte explained. "With you inside her."

"So what is that supposed to mean?" Maddy challenged.

"It means," Charlotte said flatly, "Dead Ed."

Maddy had skipped it the first time, but the prospect definitely intrigued her. Whether it was the opportunity to clean up her act or corrupt a whole new group of people, even she wasn't sure.

"Rules are rules," Pam chuckled, the tiniest tinge of vengefulness in her tone.

"Time for a little rehab for the soul, sister," Prue added with a sinister laugh.

Maddy relented and the girls let her up.

She then left the office with Beth, Mary, and Sally to begin her journey and pursue her higher afterlife education.

"You realize she's not salvageable," Prue commented to Charlotte and Pam.

"Look who's talking," Charlotte said. "Either way, at least we got her out of our world for a while."

"You can't change the world all at once," Pam proclaimed.

"But maybe, little by little," Charlotte said to her friends. "Now, if there is nothing else, I'd like to go…to prom."

Chapter 23

Some Great Reward

Tell me, who am I without you, by my side.
—George Harrison

Making up is hard to do.

Like a Call Waiting signal buzzing in your brain, the prospect of getting back together with an ex often means putting your anger, disappointment, and sometimes even your better judgment on hold to answer your heart's call. Whether it's the right party or a wrong number is hard to know unless you pick up.

s they made their way back through the corridor to the gymnasium, Charlotte thought about the lesson she was taking away from all this. Maybe the whole point of the trip was to convince her that things were no longer about her, and that she was around for the purpose of truly serving others. She had to let go of her earthly friendships and more importantly, let go of love.

Charlotte was trapped in her own reverie and looking for an escape hatch when she heard a familiar voice booming down the hall.

"Did I miss something?" Petula asked as she grabbed her ticket from the counter girl and eyed the last throes of the commotion that had preceded her.

The girl, not realizing that for Petula it was a rhetorical question, began to breathlessly relate the events of the past hour or so about Darcy collapsing, the ambulance, all of it.

"No?" Petula interrupted, heading heedlessly on her way into prom. "Good."

She was surrounded by a crowd, but not the high schoolers that typically attended her. Those days were long gone, though her haughtiness clearly was not. Whether this was just an act of self-preservation given how she'd been treated or an actual

personality backslide, the confidence that she'd been doling out to others had definitely made a comeback in her own life.

As she approached the gym doors, the ushers eyed the mob behind her suspiciously, but Petula just played them off as if she was entering a hot club where she knew all the bouncers. The difference, she always knew, between A-Listers and everyone else was not fame or fortune, but attitude.

"They're with me," she advised, giving them a "you know who I am" face and turning to wave the mini-horde, now including Pam, Prue, and Charlotte, in behind her.

Just as she was about to enter, the lights went down. Petula took this as a gesture of respect for her appearance at her last-ever high school dance.

"Hello," the announcer said. "Is everyone having a good time?"

As the lights came up everyone noticed a group of people come in all at once by the stage door. Damen brought the music down along with the lights and kept the volume low as he tried to figure out what was happening at the door.

"Oh, we have some latecomers," the announcer said. "Just in time for the main attraction!"

"I am the main attraction," Petula said as she entered, looking perfect in her gorgeous vintage Chanel gown.

Petula walked through the crowd to stunned silence, not so much because of her arrival but because she looked absolutely breathtaking. Everyone whispered about how great she looked, which ate The Wendys alive. Despite their efforts, Petula's popularity had metastasized and spread.

They whispered also about the group dragging behind her. They were her clients, as she sometimes called them, the home-

less people that she had been styling for months. They were all dressed fabulously in black, mostly pieces from Scarlet's old wardrobe, which fit in perfectly with the fantasy funeral theme. And, since it was in honor of Charlotte Usher, a girl who was also invisible, they really felt as if they belonged.

"Please, Petula," Wendy Anderson jokingly begged, pretending to hold out an empty bowl, "may I have some more."

"She doesn't have a date," Wendy Thomas howled, breaking down in hysterics. "She has a bread line."

"Yes, she does," a guy they didn't recognize said to them.

He was dressed in an expensive Armani suit. He was tan and his hair was full and coiffed. He was every girl's dream, a little disheveled, and bad-boy, but very charming. The Wendys swooned over him as he walked by them. He looked like a Hollywood actor, much too good for their little pond.

The mystery man walked over to the MC and asked for his microphone. He took it and made his way to the center of the room and motioned for Petula to join him. Damen smiled and pulled up the gain on his mic so everyone could hear.

"Who is…," Wendy Thomas stammered, "that?"

As she got closer to him, Petula found it hard to believe what she was seeing.

"Tate?" Petula sighed.

"You did invite me to your prom, didn't you?" he asked, even the cadence of his words now revealing a breeding they hadn't before.

"Yeah, but I didn't think you were going to show," she said, still confused. "And I certainly didn't think you would show like this."

"That's what I like about you," he said. "You liked me because of me, not because I'm an oil heir."

This was the first time Petula had ever been publicly accused of sincerity. She was happy to plead guilty.

"*He's* a bum?" Wendy Anderson asked, perplexed.

"He's a billionaire!" Wendy Thomas repeated, punching Wendy Anderson in the arm to quiet her.

"Why were you on the street?" she asked.

"All I seemed to attract were fame seekers, and I was sick of it," Tate explained. "I started to believe that those were the only kind of girls I would ever meet."

"What other kind are there?" Wendy Anderson asked Wendy Thomas, who just shook her head in wonder.

"I figured the only way to change that was to change everything," Tate continued. "I gave up the lifestyle, the money, and the comforts, all of it."

"Then why are you here?" Petula quizzed, cataloging his outfit loudly in an effort to make The Wendys even more jealous. "In a gorgeous, Italian designer, fine wool, single-breasted, two-button suit?"

"I was looking for something that I found when I met you," Tate said sweetly. "Now I can be me again."

Petula was once again the envy of the school and The Wendys, only this time she'd truly earned what she had. Tate handed back the mic and leaned in for a long kiss.

"Too bad CoCo isn't here for this," Pam said to Prue and Charlotte. "She did a great job."

The crowd applauded, especially the ones who'd made fun of her and brought her down. There was a certain comfort they felt having Petula as their leader, even if they envied and hated her. She never failed to deliver on giving them something to talk about.

"Now that the young lady has gotten her surprise," the announcer said, "I have one for the rest of you."

Everyone screamed, even though they had absolutely no idea who or what they were screaming for.

"As some of you may know, we had a songwriting contest at INDY-Ninety-five and the winner got to pick anywhere in town to perform their song…

"Well…she picked here!"

The crowd erupted into sheer mania.

"Part of the winning package was that she got to choose the prom theme," he added. "You have her to thank for this spectacular, otherworldly display."

Once again, the crowd roared their approval, all except The Wendys, who felt nauseated. Charlotte couldn't believe what she was hearing. The lights came down and a spotlight hit the stage, causing an even wilder reaction.

"Here she is," the announcer announced, "Hawthorne's own Scarlet Kensington."

Scarlet came out onstage, and it was apparent that she had "it." She owned the room instantly, but most of all she commanded Damen's attention. He nearly fell to his knees when he saw her up there. She appeared so beautiful and radiant in the spotlight. Her hair was up, her bangs were shiny and polished, and she was wearing a billowy black off-the-shoulder chiffon dress with some gathered gray tulle peeking out around the bust and subtly lining the bottom. Her lips were matte red and her hair was fixed in a strategic, messy updo. Damen wasn't the only one, however, who believed he was watching the birth of a star.

Scarlet draped her guitar on and looked around the room,

as much as she could see through the stage lights and darkness. She wanted to take it all in. It seemed to her that with the exception of The Wendys, everyone got the memo about dark attire. As she looked out into the sea of black, she saw Charlotte standing there in awe. Then she looked over at the DJ booth and saw Damen, alone, watching her every move.

She smiled at him.

He smiled back.

Scarlet thanked everybody, but gushed with special gratitude for one in particular.

"I want to thank Eric Smash—or as his friends know him, Electric Eric—for working with me on this song," Scarlet said. "He is a true rock star for doing this and he's here with me tonight, in spirit."

Eric took a long, deep bow and drank in the applause from the crowd, who couldn't see him, and from his friends— especially Charlotte—who could. He kissed his fingers and pointed at Charlotte to let her know this one was just for her. Pam and Prue nudged her, as she smiled, somewhat embarrassed, but secretly loving it.

"This song is based on a note I got from a very special someone, who enlisted the help of a very special other someone to write it," Scarlet announced as she strummed her guitar into the song.

"She did read it," Damen muttered.

"Charlotte Usher and Damen Dylan, this is for you!"

Silence fell over the crowd. Scarlet sang and played her guitar and Eric accompanied her. Everyone, including Damen, just assumed she was playing along with a track, but when he looked at his soundboard, hers was not the only hot channel.

Wherever that beautiful fretwork was coming from, Damen thought, it was definitely live.

"This song is called 'Kiss Your Kiss,'" Scarlet said as she sang out the first rich, melodic note.

> THOUGHT I KISSED YOUR KISS AWAY
>
> THOUGHT I LOVED YOUR LOVE TODAY
>
> SEE THE THINGS YOU SEE MY WAY
>
> I THOUGHT I KISSED YOUR KISS AWAY

Damen was transfixed not only by her presence but by what was coming out of her mouth. She was as gifted a songwriter as she was a girlfriend, he thought, singing like a seasoned performer who'd been doing it her whole life. He never saw her so comfortable. It was obvious that she belonged in front of people, playing her music, and he was even more amazed by the fact that it was all for him.

> SAID SOME THINGS I SHOULDN'T SAY,
>
> NEEDED YOUR NEED TO STAY
>
> SEE THE THINGS YOU SEE MY WAY
>
> DID I KISS YOUR KISS AWAY?

> I CAN'T HELP BUT THINK WHEN YOU'RE AWAY FROM ME,
>
> YOU ARE MY MEANT-TO-BE.

She sang that bridge with her soul, and Eric played the guitar like a virtuoso, able to evoke emotions and tell a story with his chords and progressions. He was where he belonged up

there, his life cut too short, and now he was getting his chance, all because of Scarlet. Charlotte was swept away by him; it was as if he was explaining everything to her with just his music. If she wasn't in love with him before, she was now.

For the last verse, Scarlet walked over to the side of the stage where Damen was watching her from the DJ booth and fixed her eyes on him. She sang the words right to him, and everyone in the room felt their intense energy. Eric walked over to the other side of the stage where Charlotte was standing. He played only for her, and it was clear how Eric felt: he was telling her.

> I THOUGHT I KISSED YOUR KISS AWAY
> THOUGHT I LOVED YOUR LOVE TODAY
> CAN ONLY WISH, HOPE, AND PRAY
> TO NEVER KISS YOUR KISS AWAY.

> I CAN'T HELP BUT THINK WHEN YOU'RE AWAY FROM ME,
> STRAIGHT FROM THE HEART OF A MEANT-TO-BE.

As she continued the song, Damen took off, running toward the stage. As soon as he jumped up, Scarlet was winding up with a big finish. The crowd was out of control, and so was Damen. He grabbed Scarlet to massive appreciative applause.

"I'm sorry," he said, holding her in his arms.

"Me too," she said, smiling, before their moment was interrupted.

"Wow! Looks like we have a rising star right here at Hawthorne High tonight," the announcer said. "Now, let's see who the star of the prom is!"

The Wendys ran to the stage, eager to hear the results, anticipating their night to shine. If one of them got Prom Queen, it could be just the thing they needed to start their brand-new future. Like an injured racehorse, Darcy, they figured, had to be scratched, and Scarlet would never allow her name to be placed in the running. It would be between the two of them and Petula, and she had taken such a public beating before voting had concluded that it was hard to imagine her as the winner. It had to be one of them.

Damen, now back at the DJ booth, only this time with Scarlet on his arm, hit the drum-roll sound effect and the lights dimmed. The Wendys held each other tightly, their eyes shut as they hung on every breath the announcer took.

"And your queen is…"

"It will be you," Wendy Anderson said, grasping Wendy Thomas's hand.

"No, it will definitely be you," Wendy Thomas said, almost breaking skin from the anticipation.

"Petula Kensington!"

The roar of surprise rattled the rafters. Apparently, Petula had a few fans left.

"How in the world did that happen?" Wendy Anderson protested.

Even Petula was stunned.

The room exploded in applause and catcalls, text messages, and cell phone flashes.

"Is this high school," Wendy Thomas screamed in frustration, "or hell?"

"Voter fraud!" Wendy Anderson howled, nearly apoplectic. "Somebody call the U.N.!"

Charlotte looked over and saw Virginia giggling at the ballot box, and suddenly it made sense.

"Looks like Petula's new guide arrived," Charlotte said to Eric, even though he had no idea what she was talking about.

"We're done here," Pam said proudly, pleased at The Wendys' comeuppance.

"We were done here," Prue added, taking her buddy's hand, "a long time ago."

Petula Kensington was queen, and everything was as it should be.

Pam and Prue flashed Virginia a thumbs-up and made for the exit.

As the pipe organ music started to play, a group of dapper football players dressed as pallbearers came and picked Petula and Tate up, and carried the happy couple away in open caskets.

ॐ

"Let's go dance," Scarlet said, grabbing Charlotte's hand and looking around for Damen. She was standing behind the large speaker cabinets and out of view.

"No," Charlotte said gently, pointing to Damen, who was walking through the crowd toward her. "You've got someone to dance with. And so do I."

"Are you still angry with me?" Scarlet asked, a little hurt.

"How could I be after all this?" Charlotte gestured around the room.

Eric came up to join them, and Scarlet turned to him to say her goodbye.

"Thanks for letting me totally be myself around you," she

said, "so that I could prove to myself that Damen would accept me no matter what."

"No sweat," Eric said simply. "That's what I was here for. Rock on."

Scarlet hiked up her dress and exposed a pair of the coolest combat boots ever designed—both were adorned with hundreds of tiny black rhinestones to match her dress and laced up with gorgeous vintage gray satin bows.

"The official ruby slipper of the rebel."

Eric smiled, taking her choice in shoes as both a compliment and a victory.

Scarlet grabbed Charlotte's hands. "It's been quite a ride," she said.

"You've still got a long way to go," Charlotte said encouragingly. "You've got your whole life ahead of you."

For Scarlet, the comment was bittersweet, because Charlotte was right. She had her whole life ahead of her, but Charlotte didn't.

"It's funny, you wanted to disappear and I wanted to be seen," Charlotte noted. "Now, all I want is to disappear from here, and you are definitely going to be seen by millions someday."

Damen took a break from the DJ booth and walked over to Scarlet.

"I could never have been myself without you," Scarlet said to Charlotte, but just as she did, Charlotte strategically disappeared. So Scarlet actually ended up saying it to Damen instead.

Suddenly, she found herself in his arms. Damen pulled her in close for a kiss that was all their own.

Epilogue

I Will Follow You into the Dark

No blinding light or tunnels to gates of white
Just our hands clasped so tight
—Death Cab for Cutie

You never know.

———◆◆◆———

We all have ideas about love and death. We keep a close eye out for them our entire lives, seeking one and avoiding the other, knowing all the while that both are mostly beyond our control. It is a both scary and exciting predicament. In the end, it all depends on how you look at it. One thing is for sure; it is never quite what you expect.

It was a misty dawn and the anxious sun began to push the night up like a yellowing, antique window shade, unleashing a flood of morning light. Everyone had left the prom and was going to the diner for an early breakfast before heading back to their warm beds to sleep the day away.

Damen was about to drop Scarlet off when she turned to him and kissed his cheek lightly.

"Tonight was amazing," Scarlet purred.

"You're amazing," Damen said, grabbing her hand.

The change they were feeling inside had finally come, not to break them apart but to bring them even closer together.

Damen got out and opened Scarlet's door gallantly. He wasn't dropping her off at her house like all the other guys, but then again, nothing about their relationship even remotely resembled anyone else's.

Scarlet got out, gathered her gown, and made her way through the marshy ground, toward the monument.

"I'll call you later," he said as he watched her hair glisten in the morning light.

The cemetery was a peaceful place, but especially so in the early morning. Not even the animals were awake yet, so it was more than just quiet. It was silent, except for the familiar voice blending in the breeze as she approached the headstone.

Just as Scarlet hoped, Charlotte was waiting for her.

"I forgot to tell you," Charlotte said. "Your song was beautiful."

"Thanks," Scarlet replied. "I couldn't have done it without Eric."

"Eric's something else, isn't he?" Charlotte said.

"He's a great guy," Scarlet advised. "Don't lose him."

"Right back at you," Charlotte said, smiling.

"I ended up with the prep, and you ended up with the rocker," Scarlet said. "Ironic, isn't it?"

"Can't help who you fall in love with," Charlotte said.

The graveyard was a strange place for a bull session, but under the circumstances, there was something totally right about it.

"The radio station is going to release our song as a single," Scarlet said. "I'm going to put Eric's name on it with mine," she said. "Kind of an audio memorial to him."

"I'll tell him," Charlotte said. "He'll die."

"And all the proceeds will go to the homeless," Scarlet added.

"I'll bet Petula is excited about that," Charlotte said with a smile.

"That," Scarlet added, "and her new boyfriend."

"Of course," Charlotte said. "Same old Petula."

"Well, not quite," Scarlet joked, acknowledging her sister's evolution. "Thankfully."

Charlotte knew what she meant, and they both shared a laugh.

"Tell her she's got a little beauty queen on her shoulder now," Charlotte offered. "Her very own guardian angel."

"Virginia?" Scarlet sighed happily, knowing how much Virginia's presence would mean to Petula.

There had been a lot of awkward silences between them this time, like they were talking on satellite delay, but it was not for want of things to say. It was their unspoken way of stretching the moments, slowing things down, making each second with each other last as long as possible.

"This is the start of it," Charlotte said. "You're going to be a star."

"I thought you were a ghost, not a prophet," Scarlet said, smiling appreciatively. "It's just a local station."

"There's nothing local about you," Charlotte said.

Scarlet nodded and then more silence followed.

Scarlet felt so grateful that they'd found each other and that Charlotte had found love, not just with her parents, but with Eric too.

"Will I ever talk to you again?" Scarlet asked, sensing the end was near.

"Scarlet, I lived my life, now it's time you lived yours," Charlotte said. "This is your time, your memories now."

"Please don't…," Scarlet pleaded.

"I love you Scarlet," Charlotte said, unwilling to say goodbye.

"I love you too," Scarlet said, embracing Charlotte.

Charlotte smiled and started humming the melody to Scarlet's song, only in a more mournful way, as she turned to her monument. It was eerily beautiful, how she sounded, how she moved; it was otherworldly. Before Scarlet could say another word, Charlotte solemnly walked into the bust Scarlet had commissioned, bringing it to life for a brief moment, and then sank into her grave, the melancholy dirge echoing in the wind.

"Rest in peace, my friend," Scarlet said, dropping to her knees and this time letting her tears fall to the grass on Charlotte's grave.

❧

Charlotte woke up to her mother calling her. She shifted back and forth in her bed, trying to sleep off her Hawthorne High hangover.

"Honey, your friend is here," her mother said, knowing that was just the alarm clock she needed.

Charlotte shot out of bed and tried to make herself presentable.

"Hey," Eric said.

Charlotte was so happy to see him. He'd come to pick her up, just like a real boyfriend would.

"Mom, Dad," Charlotte said, taking a deep breath. "This is Eric."

"You know," Eileen said, "Charlotte told me that Scarlet once said that if anyone could find love over here, it's Charlotte. What do you think about that?"

"I think she's right," Eric said.

Even Charlotte's dad couldn't keep a smile from breaking out, as he gave Eric an approving slap on the back.

After saying their goodbyes, Eric and Charlotte walked hand-in-hand to the call center, for what they hoped would be the last time.

Prue, Pam, and all the others waited anxiously for Charlotte to get there. They wanted to be there to support her, knowing just how hard it was for her to say goodbye to Scarlet.

"I never thought the departed had to deal with missing their loved ones," Pam said sympathetically.

Charlotte forced a smile, with a little help from the hand squeeze Eric gave her.

Green Gary, Polly, Lipo Lisa, Paramour Polly, ADD Andy, and the rest of their intern class were seated and waiting patiently for the little "moving on" ceremony for Charlotte's crew to conclude, so that they could get back to the phones. They'd overheard the stories from the returning spirits and they knew someday, for lack of a better way to say it, they'd get their assignments and their chance to make a difference too.

Markov came into the room just as everyone's patience was at the breaking point.

Charlotte smiled, this time more easily.

"So, did you have a nice trip?" Markov asked her.

She wanted to get into all the details of the journey, but kept it simple instead. Something she knew he would appreciate.

"It's something how people think angels are sent to earth to help them," Charlotte began. "It's just as much the living helping the angels though."

"Eternity with a twist," Markov joked knowingly.

"It's been a real pleasure working for you," Charlotte said respectfully. "I'll never forget what I learned here."

"I expect you won't," Markov replied, pleased that he'd gotten through to her and to all of them in the end.

"We'll miss you," the interns called out in unison, as they prepared to scatter.

"Good luck to all of you," Markov said. "You may go and so, finally, may I."

Charlotte's class hugged and laughed, a mixture of happiness and relief that their job was finally done and that they were leaving the call center in good hands.

"Everyone except for Usher," a familiar voice called out unexpectedly.

Charlotte felt her heart sink, and then fill to nearly bursting as she turned to see Mr. Brain. Just as she'd hoped, his old class's departure was a special enough occasion for him to attend.

"Everyone," Brain said, getting the new interns' attention. "May I present to you your new instructor, Charlotte Usher," he said. "I know she's taught me a lot."

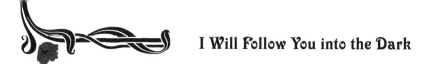

Charlotte was so honored by the appointment, but most of all she was honored to have finally found the love and the life she'd always wanted.

The end?

Acknowledgments

I would like to thank the following from the bottom of my heart:

Isabelle Rose Pagnotta, my biggest dream come true.
Oscar Martin, for making my life an adventure.
My mother, Beverly Hurley, for all of her love, dedication, and sacrifices.
My twin sister and partner, Tracy Hurley Martin, for believing in everything I do, whether she should or not.
My father, Tom Hurley, for teaching me how to fight.
My grandparents Martha and Anthony Kolencik for teaching me how to love and to be loved.
My undying gratitude to my editor, Nancy Conescu, whose enthusiasm and support have made all of this possible.

Special thanks to all who have helped bring *ghostgirl* to life: Craig Phillips, Megan Tingley, Lawrence Mattis, Andy McNicol, Alison Impey, Andrea Spooner, Lisa Sabater, Lisa Ickowicz, Lauren Hodge, Tracy Fisher, Melanie Chang, Amy Verardo, Andrew Smith, Tina McIntyre, Jonathan Lopes, Shawn Foster, Chris Murphy, Salvatore and Mary Pagnotta, Denise Carlo, Tom Hurley, Haley Gaydos, Mary Nemchik, Lauren Nemchik, Deborah Bilitski, Clemmie Morton, Vincent Martin, Jean Piazza, and Theresa Flaherty.

Tonya Hurley made her debut with **ghostgirl**, which was an instant *New York Times* bestseller. Her credits span all platforms of teen entertainment: creating, writing, and producing two hit TV series; writing and directing several acclaimed independent films; and developing a groundbreaking collection of video games. Ms. Hurley lives in New York with her husband and daughter. Visit her award-winning website at **www.ghostgirl.com**.